'I—don't know,' Anthea said slowly.

What *did* she say? Could she spend two weeks in Charles's company without ending up completely besotted with him? And what would that bring her? Nothing but black misery. He'd been honest with her.

His eyes were fixed on her, and it seemed that he was following at least part of her train of thought.

'I admit I'm being entirely selfish,' he said. 'I should very much enjoy your company. But of course if you're looking for a——'

'A sexual romp? I'm not,' Anthea said coolly.

DEEP
WATER

BY

MARJORIE LEWTY

MILLS & BOON LIMITED
ETON HOUSE   18-24 PARADISE ROAD
RICHMOND   SURREY   TW9 1SR

First published in Great Britain 1991 by Mills & Boon Limited

© Marjorie Lewty 1991

Australian copyright 1991 Philippine copyright 1992 This edition 1992

ISBN 0 263 77304 3

Set in Times Roman 10½ on 12 pt. 91-9202-51731 C

Made and printed in Great Britain

CHAPTER ONE

SHE was sitting in the transit lounge of Miami airport when she saw him again. It was five years ago, but she recognised him at once.

He was leaning against a pillar, a tall, dark, faintly-bored-looking man, probably in his mid-thirties. He held a newspaper in his hand, but she didn't think he was reading it. Every now and again he'd look up, frowning, at the departures board, then his glance would pass without interest over the occupants of the rows of seats. Once it passed over her, but it didn't pause for an instant. Why should it? He wouldn't recognise the pale, tired-looking girl in the smart taupe travelling suit as the shy seventeen-year-old he'd befriended at a wedding party five years ago.

Charles, she thought. She'd never heard his other name and she hadn't wanted to enquire.

Charles. It suited him. Suited his tall, spare, muscular frame in its expensively tailored dark suit. He'd worn a white dinner jacket that other evening and that had seemed swooningly romantic to her then. What a naïve child she must have been!

Now, in this airport lounge halfway across the world, she stared at him and to her amazement felt a faint stirring low inside her. A hangover from five years ago? Or merely a frank female reaction to a man whose sexual magnetism was so immediately evident? His black hair had threads of white over the ears now, she saw, which gave him an even more distinguished appearance. A captain of industry, no doubt about that. Five years ago that wouldn't have worried her, but now it would. Geoffrey was a financial wizard, as were all his friends, and she had had more than enough of financial wizards in the last few months.

She amused herself by wondering how the man standing by the pillar would react if she went up to him and said, 'Hello, Charles—remember me? I'm Anthea Lloyd—we met at my sister Pamela's wedding party in London, ages ago.'

He would, she thought, be polite and hide his dismay and boredom. He was too kind to give her a brush-off. She remembered his kindness that night of the party. He hadn't *had* to rescue a shy young girl, lost among the sophisticated friends of her elder sister and her new brother-in-law.

Suddenly she felt her body brace itself to rise from the seat—as if some outside force were pulling her towards him. Then she saw him fold his newspaper, thrust it impatiently into a litter bin and become lost to view as he strode off through the crowd towards the information desk. She sank back into her seat, rather devastated to find that she was trembling all over. A few minutes later, when she boarded her plane to Grand Cayman, her knees still felt weak. But that, she told herself, was because she really was tired out. Nothing to do with a memory of a teenage crush.

The flight from Heathrow to Miami had seemed endless, but now there was only about another hour to go. She laid her head back and looked down at the dark blue of the sea below and tried to feel thrilled and excited that she would soon be having a luxury holiday on a luxury island.

She *would* be thrilled and excited when she got there and saw Pamela again, after nearly two years. But just now all she felt was a dragging tiredness.

She wrenched her thoughts away from the traumas of the last months and centred them on the here and now.

How odd that she should see Charles again after all this time! Even odder that she should recognise him without any doubt in her mind. It was ages since she'd given him a thought, but now she found the memory coming back to her, vivid and detailed, of that strange little meeting five years ago at Pamela's wedding party.

Five years ago... Anthea closed her eyes and drifted into a half-sleep, lulled by the distant throb of the engines. And then she was back in that riverside apartment in London. She was seventeen and she was wearing a pink jersey dress which she'd designed and made herself. It had long, fitted sleeves, a soft, flutey skirt and a wide belt with a silver clasp, and she'd been rather pleased with it—until she saw the clothes the other women were wearing. Now she was feeling awkward and self-conscious among a roomful of smart and sophisticated strangers.

Pamela and Guy had left for their honeymoon an hour ago, but the party in Guy's London apartment was dragging on. There was plenty of food and drink left and the guests had evidently decided to make an evening of it.

She stood alone beside the long window opening on to the balcony, and her palms were beginning to feel damp with nerves. She didn't know any of the other guests and they weren't taking any notice of her.

Her father had been spirited away to another room by Guy's father, presumably to get some peace.

In the long, elegant drawing-room, someone put on a record and, as the September light began to fade, the room was soon full of gyrating couples.

Presently she slipped out on to the balcony and leant on the railings, watching the dusk settling mistily over the Thames and the river-boats gliding silently along. It was all rather beautiful, she thought with pleasure, the air cool on her cheeks. Lovely to get away from the noise and heat inside the room. She could stay here until Daddy came to fetch her. She was rather glad that her stepmother had had one of her migraines and hadn't come to London for the wedding. Neither she nor Pamela had much in common with their father's new wife.

She didn't hear the man come up behind her until he spoke. 'Why all alone out here?' he said, and his voice was deep and quizzical, like the voices of the heroes in the Regency romances she loved.

She glanced sideways and upwards, but couldn't see his face clearly. It was easier not to feel shy when she didn't have to meet the politely bored expression on the faces of Guy's city friends.

'Because I'm a wallflower,' she answered, adding with a grin, 'If you're familiar with the term. And because I like it out here.'

He moved forward and stood beside her, his tall body a dark shadow against the paling sky. His head was close to hers as he rested his forearms on the rail. 'I like it here too,' he said. 'And I rather like wallflowers. They bloom in May and herald the summer, and they smell nice.' He leaned towards her. 'Mmm— you smell nice too.'

Her stomach lurched. What was this—was he going to kiss her? Suddenly she felt very young and inexperienced. It wasn't because she'd never been kissed, but this man was in a different league from the boys at tennis club dances, and she guessed that his kisses would be different too. She felt a *frisson* of something that might be fear in the pit of her stomach. When he drew away again she felt relief—or could it be disappointment?

'Who are you—what's your real name, little wallflower?' he said. 'Heavens, that sounds like something from Gilbert and Sullivan.'

She laughed, suddenly relaxed. 'I know.' She sang softly, '"I'm called Little Buttercup, dear little Buttercup, though I could never tell why..."'

'Very nice,' he said. '*Pinafore*, isn't it? We share an enthusiasm, do we?'

'I love Gilbert and Sullivan,' she replied eagerly. 'I've got all the records.' She added a little sadly, 'They were my mother's—all old LPs.'

'Not very fashionable. Don't you go in for pop or rock or whatever the latest thing is?' he asked, not with superior amusement but almost as if he wanted to know.

'Oh, those too—a few,' she admitted.

'But you haven't told me who you are and why you're here,' he said.

'I'm merely the bride's kid sister. Nobody, really.'

He swung round with his back to the railings, so that the light from the room fell full on his face. Her heart skipped a beat. He was so dark and—not exactly handsome, but—somehow *exciting*. Just meeting the gleam of his eyes beneath their lowered lids made her feel very odd inside in a way she'd never felt before.

'Oh, no,' he said softly. 'Not "merely". And certainly not "nobody". Even in this light I can see that you're going to break a lot of male hearts very soon.'

'Me?' she croaked, overcome. 'You're just being kind, aren't you?'

He chuckled, a sound deep in his throat. 'Oh, I'm always reasonably kind, I hope, to little children and dumb animals, but you don't come into either category, so you must believe that I'm being truthful. You're very lovely, and that's a beautiful dress you're wearing. Is one allowed to kiss the bride's sister?'

He leaned down and kissed her gently on the lips. His hair brushed her forehead and her heart gave a great throb and bounced about crazily. When he drew away she put a hand up to her throat in case he should see the way the bodice of her pink jersey dress was straining against her breasts.

This immediate awareness of a strange man was new and overwhelming. But of course he wasn't like any man she'd ever met before—ever even seen, for that matter. He was as different from the boys she knew as—as a jungle leopard from a domestic tabby. He was dark—and dangerous—and utterly devastating.

'Come and sit down and tell me about yourself,' he said, and drew her to a wooden seat beside the wall. 'I take it you've left school? What next?'

'I'm starting at college soon, here in London,' she told him, 'studying fashion design.'

He nodded. 'And you live at home?'

'My home's in the Midlands, but I'm going to share a flat in London with two other girls.' Suddenly she found herself talking easily, telling him about her widower father's having married again recently, and about her stepmother, who didn't fancy having a grown-up stepdaughter around the house. 'I suppose you can understand that, really,' she said rather wistfully. And about her sister Pamela, six years older, who had just got married and was so amazingly beautiful...

'But, of course, you know Pamela,' she said, suddenly becoming self-conscious again.

'Not really—Guy is a colleague of my sister's husband at the bank.' He laughed. He had a gorgeous, deep laugh, and it sent little shivers down her back. 'I'm gate-crashing the party, actually.'

The music changed to a slow, smoochy beat. Inside the room the lights were dimmed. Couples clung together, rocking on the spot or moving languidly like figures in a film dream-sequence.

The man turned towards the open door into the drawing-room. He's leaving me, Anthea thought, and felt as if she were slipping into a great black hole.

But he held out a hand to her. 'Come and dance with me, little wallflower,' he said, and she went into his arms as if it was the most natural thing in the world to be pressed against him, to move with him to the heavy beat of the music, her head against his shoulder, her body soft and pliant, and a slow warmth creeping all over her.

'Charles!'

A vision in glittery white, smooth and perfumed, came between them in the dim light, sliding one arm possessively round the man's neck. 'Darling, I'm so sorry I couldn't make the start of the party, but I thought you might still be here. Have you had enough—shall we go back to my flat?' The light voice dropped huskily on the last words.

'Cherry, my sweet!' They were kissing now, at length, like lovers.

She ought to have expected it; she should have known he had a girl—probably lots of girls. But the shattering of the dream was so sudden, so brutal. Shivering, she turned and began to grope her way towards the door. She must find her father—tell him she wanted to leave. But the close mass of swaying bodies barred her way.

Charles's arm shot out and caught her.

'We were dancing,' he said. 'Remember?' He added, to the girl in white, 'Wait in the car for me, sweetheart; I'll be with you soon.'

The girl he'd called Cherry—or was it *chérie*?— laughed lightly. 'OK, I'll leave you to your duty-dance, darling. But don't be long.'

This was the worst of all—to be looked upon as a duty. 'Please...' she stammered as his arms closed round her again. 'You don't have to—it was kind of you but ... but really I'm OK. I must go and find my father.'

'*Really?*' His voice was faintly teasing.

'Yes, really.' She drew away and felt as if she was going to burst into tears. 'Thank you for taking pity on me,' she muttered, not looking at him, and pushed her way desperately between the clinging couples into the hall ...

Gradually the scene faded. Anthea was back again in the plane, and her eyes were full of tears. She was aware of the beat of the engines and the smiling stewardess beside her with a tray of coffee.

She blinked at the girl stupidly. 'Oh, thank you. Yes, coffee, please.'

She laid her head back against the seat, part of her mind still back in that other scene, five years ago, marvelling that the sight of the man called Charles should have recalled that small episode in such detail. But perhaps it wasn't so strange. At the time she had engraved it on her memory—on her heart. She hadn't allowed herself to forget Charles. She'd thought about him all through the two years at college. She'd come across a photograph of him in a glossy magazine, taken in a group at some millionaire's house-party, and had cut it out, isolating him from the surrounding people, and hung it on the wall of her bedroom. The names were under the photograph, but the print was too blurred to decipher. She was rather glad. He was . . . just Charles.

Whereas the other girls had had pin-ups of pop stars and racing drivers, she had had Charles. Her pin-up. And, although she'd giggled at the absurdity of it, she'd allowed herself to fantasise over him now and then. He'd seemed to her youthful idealism like the perfect man, and she'd endowed him with all the qualities she especially liked: humour, kindness, generosity, broad-mindedness—he had the lot, as well as being tall and gorgeous to look at. And even now, after all this time, she remembered how his brief, friendly kiss had jolted her into a knowledge of her own sexuality.

Five years ago! And the magnetism was still there. She had almost made a fool of herself in the airport lounge. Ah, well, ships that pass in the night, she thought, with a rueful smile for the romantic girl she'd been at seventeen. She was hardly likely to encounter her pin-up again. She gazed through the plane's window at the blue sea below and turned her thoughts to the happiness of seeing Pamela, and to the holiday ahead.

That night, in her sister's luxury condo on Seven Mile Beach in Grand Cayman, Anthea slept round the clock. Jet lag, plus the after-effects of a dose of flu, plus the worries and disasters of the last two months, had left her feeling like a washed-out rag. She hadn't realised how tired she'd been. Sleep was what she needed most.

She opened her eyes and closed them again quickly. Just lately, waking up had been something she'd put off as long as possible. There'd been no promise of a glad new day when she'd awakened to the dismal January light that had seeped in through the window of her London flat.

But now something was different. Filtered sunlight was caressing her eyelids; a warm, scented breeze was fanning her cheeks; a softly-sprung mattress was moulding itself seductively to her slim body.

Cautiously she opened her eyes again and lifted herself up on to one elbow. The bedroom was a dream. White slatted blinds at the wide window let through narrow bars of sunshine, falling across the sleek ivory furniture, the pale green carpet, the silky multi-coloured bedspread that covered her to the waist. Through a half-open door she could see the pale green fitments of a connecting shower-room.

A smile began to pull at the corners of her mouth. Of course—the Caribbean! To be exact, the Cayman Islands, that paradise of the rich and successful. Anthea wasn't rich, or successful, but Pamela was both, and that was how she had come to be here.

The door opened a crack and then swung fully open, and her sister came in, a white wrap drifting round her, her wonderful golden hair loose around her beautiful face—the face that, until her marriage, had appeared on the covers of most of the glossy magazines in the Western world. She was smiling, and carrying a small tray.

'Thea—you're awake at last, my poppet. You've had a lovely sleep—how are you feeling now? You were absolutely all in when you arrived yesterday. I tucked you up in bed straight away.'

Anthea pulled herself up against the pillows, smiling and stretching her arms above her head. 'I'm in heaven, of course, so I feel marvellous.'

Pamela came across the room, put down the tray to give Anthea a hug, and sat on the side of the bed. Six months of pregnancy hadn't changed her dazzling beauty—only, it seemed, added to the dazzle.

She studied Anthea's pale face, frowning slightly. 'Darling, it's marvellous to have you here. But you really have been taking a beating, haven't you? Sweetie, you look rotten. What's been happening? I've been marooned here in the Caymans without news of you. You haven't written for ages—not since you wrote to tell me about that awful fire at the warehouse and losing all your stock.'

There was no doubt about the two girls' being sisters. But Anthea had sometimes thought that if Pamela could be viewed in Technicolor then she herself might be a sepia edition. Her own hair was as fine and lustrous, but, whereas Pamela's was a rich corn-gold, hers was the brown of autumn beech leaves. Pamela's eyes were dazzling blue; Anthea's were a darker blue, shading to violet. Pamela's cheeks were tanned by the Caribbean sun to a pale biscuit colour. Anthea's had the pallor of England in late January.

It was just as well, Anthea thought wryly, that she had never wanted to compete. Pamela's ambitions hadn't been hers, although she loved her sister dearly.

'*Marooned*, Pam?' she scoffed. 'In this fabulous luxury condo...' she waved a hand round the bedroom '...with an adoring husband and a baby on the way, and sun and sea and sand all around? Marooned! Don't give me that!'

Pamela pulled a face. 'OK, I take back the "marooned". But you haven't answered my question. What goes on?'

Anthea shrugged. 'Oh, a dose of flu last month. Pressure of work. There's been such a lot to attend to since the fire—dealing with customers, writing dozens of letters, all the insurance to sort out and so on.' She hesitated, biting her lip and looking away. 'Geoffrey's exit from the scene. The last two items not unconnected, I may say.'

Her elder sister put in quickly, 'Oh, you poor darling, I'm so sorry. But I must admit I always thought Geoffrey Derningham was a bit of a creep. What happened?'

'He—sort of lost interest when the business folded, after the fire. When I was successful and had time to dress up and make him proud to take me out among his well-heeled friends, everything was marvellous. But after the fire I was worried, and I suppose I got a bit bothered and dismal, and he didn't want to know. When everything went up in smoke our romance did too.'

She was silent for a moment, then she firmed her lips. 'Best thing, really. If he wasn't prepared to back me up when things went wrong *before* we were married, what chance would there have been for us afterwards?'

Pamela sighed and shook her head affectionately. 'It's been a wretched break for you, poppet. I worry about you, you know. You always seem to be working too hard to have any fun. I seem to have so much and you've got——'

'Don't say I've got nothing,' Anthea put in quickly. 'It was a horrid blow about the fire, but it was just as bad for all the others who had studios and work-rooms in the warehouse. I'll find somewhere else and start again—and there's still plenty of time for fun; I'm not over the hill yet—I'm only twenty-two. But don't let's talk about me any more—how about you? You look blooming, Pam. Impending motherhood certainly suits you.'

'Yes, doesn't it? Everything's fine; Junior's coming along a treat.' Pamela's smile was radiant. 'I can recommend pregnancy—it makes you feel so beautifully important. Everyone makes a fuss of you. And now we're together again, which makes everything lovely.' She leaned over and kissed Anthea's cheek impulsively, and a breath of French perfume wafted on the warm air. 'I've missed my little sister.'

Then she drew back and studied Anthea's pale face thoughtfully, frowning a little. 'But I wish *you* were having a better time, Thea. All that work—setting up the business and then——'

'Don't let's talk about it,' Anthea put in quickly. 'I want to forget it; it was just one of those things.'

Pamela nodded seriously. 'You lost a lot, did you? You must have done.'

'Everything went. My new electronic knitting machines, every last bit of yarn, more than twenty finished garments. Everything.'

'Oh, gosh, that's bad.' Pamela shook her head. 'Look, if there's anything that Guy and I can do...'

Anthea held up a hand. 'Thanks, Pam, but I'll get the insurance money—eventually. Anyway, I couldn't accept any more. Paying my fare to come out here was a lovely birthday present, and I'm going to make the most of my stay and go home fighting fit.'

Pamela shook her head. 'You shouldn't have to fight. What you need is a nice rich husband to do your fighting for you.'

'Like yours?' Anthea's violet-blue eyes twinkled.

'You could do worse,' her sister said smugly. 'I'll have to find one for you while you're here.'

'Don't you dare, bossy boots! I'll find a husband for myself—if I decide I want one, that is. I'm not sure that I do.'

Not after Geoffrey. She'd been in love with Geoffrey and when he'd walked out on her it had hurt badly. It wasn't an experience she wanted to repeat.

Pamela stood up and put the tray on her sister's knees. 'Now eat your brunch like a good girl, and then we'll have a lovely lazy afternoon until Guy comes home from the bank. That OK?'

'Fine! And, Pam...'

'Mmm?'

'Thanks for everything,' Anthea said. She grinned. 'I love you. Just so long as you don't go trying to find a rich husband for me! Promise.'

Pamela looked at her and walked across to the door. Anthea knew that look of old. It meant that her sister was planning to get her own way about something.

'Promise!' Anthea wailed.

Pamela turned, pulled a face at her, and closed the door.

CHAPTER TWO

'GLAD you're here?' Pamela's voice came lazily from the green canvas lounger next to Anthea's. In the late afternoon they had the area round the private pool to themselves.

Anthea opened her eyes behind their dark sunglasses. 'Mmm—this is pure paradise.'

She let her gaze move over the scene. The three dazzling white condo buildings, each with two duplex apartments, were grouped round curving driveways. Low-growing shrubs, starred with tiny pink flowers, dotted the grass borders. In the swimming pool turquoise water glittered in the sunshine. Ahead, the feathery fronds of the casuarina trees fringing the beach formed an archway, through which she could see a rim of fine white sand leading down to a murmuring sea whose colour changed from palest green to deep, deep blue on the horizon. As she looked, the multi-coloured stripes of a tall pointed sail glided silently past. It was like looking at a brilliantly lit theatre stage.

'It really is heavenly here—just as good as you've always told me,' Anthea said dreamily. 'I don't know how you'll be able to bear to leave when the time comes.'

Pamela stretched her arms above her head and yawned. 'Oh, I don't know. We've been here for two years and one gets tired of anything in time. Sometimes I quite yearn for grimy old London and the theatres and the shops and all our friends. Not that there aren't some nice people around here too. And here's one of them—Nancy Jamieson. She and Bill were at my wedding—remember them?'

'No, I don't think I do.' Anthea's memories of the people at her sister's wedding had all faded—except for one: a tall, dark, fabulous man who had kissed her on a balcony overlooking the river.

'Bill and Nancy haven't been here long,' Pamela went on. 'Bill's in the bank with Guy. They're the nicest folk.' She lifted an arm. 'Nancy—over here!'

The woman who came towards them, smiling cheerfully, was considerably older than Pamela, forty-ish probably. She wore a jazzy beach-dress that barely covered an ample, almost matronish figure, and her dark hair was cut in a straight fringe across her forehead.

'Pamela—the very person I wanted to see.' She plonked herself down into the hammock chair next to Pamela's. 'Phew! I haven't adjusted to the climate yet. But what I wanted to say was: are you and Guy dining anywhere special tonight? If not, will you join our table at the Coconut Tree and help Bill and me to amuse my baby brother, who's descended upon us for the diving—rather unexpectedly?'

'Yes, of course, we'd love to.'

Anthea's heart sank a little; she'd hoped for a quiet evening and an early bedtime. But Pamela sounded genuinely enthusiastic. Pamela had always been a party girl. 'Never refuse an invitation,' had been her motto from schooldays; 'you never know what might turn up.'

'We'll be three,' Pamela added. 'Not just Guy and me. This is Anthea, my sister from London. Anthea, meet Nancy Jamieson. Nancy and Bill are in the club—bank people.'

Nancy leaned across and took Anthea's hand in a firm grip. 'Great! You two young things will be able to find lots to chat about and leave the old buffers to their boring shop talk.'

'Shop talk?' Pamela squeaked indignantly.

'Well, it is, isn't it?' Nancy grinned, pulling herself out of her chair with a grunt. 'Guy and Bill, deep into putting the financial world to rights, and you and I discussing baby clothes. Now I must go and see how my poor young brother is getting along. I left him on his own while I went into the town to get my hair done, and he's rather in the dumps just now.' She grimaced. 'Trouble in his love-life, I guess, although he's pretty clam-like about it. Doesn't say much. Ah, well—the miseries of youth! See you both tonight.' She gave them a cheery salute and strode away purposefully towards the middle block of the condo apartments.

Anthea slid her sister a dark look. 'You jumped at that invitation, didn't you? I wouldn't by any chance be right in suspecting that some wheels are turning in that busy little brain of yours, would I? You wouldn't be having thoughts about a certain young man whose love-life has gone wrong and who needs cheering up?'

Pamela put on an innocent look. 'You mean the bit about the "two young things" that Nancy suggested? No, cross my heart, love, I didn't even know the young brother had arrived. Nancy told me she has a young brother who works in the City, in London, but I don't think I've ever met him. It may be fun for you to have someone to play tennis with, or go diving. You'll have to learn to dive, you know.

You can't have a Caymans holiday without inspecting
the underwater scene. The colours! It's absolutely
amazing. If Nancy's young brother has come for the
diving he'll be able to give you a few lessons.'

Anthea smiled. Pam was off again—making plans,
producing young men, just as she had done in London
before Guy was moved to the Caymans. She wasn't
capable of scheming and interfering—of course she
wasn't. She simply wanted Anthea to find the right
man, as she herself had done. What she didn't realise
was that Anthea wasn't likely to find the right man
among the set that Pamela and Guy moved in. Guy
was a sweetie, and he and Pam adored each other,
but life in the fast financial lane wasn't for Anthea.
She looked for a lot more in a man than a knack for
making a great deal of money. She'd thought she'd
found it in Geoffrey. She'd been mistaken, and she
certainly didn't want to try again for a long time. But
it might be agreeable to have someone to play tennis
with—and possibly to dive with, if it wasn't too difficult to learn, and if Nancy's brother was willing to
teach her.

'OK, I'll look the young man over,' she said with
mock loftiness. 'But if he's nursing a broken heart he
doesn't sound very good company.'

Her sister laughed mischievously. 'You, my sweet,
are just the right antidote for a broken heart. You
wait and see. Now, you've had enough sun for your
first time. You have to be very careful here—something about the ultra-violet light's being especially
strong. Let's go in and have a drink all ready for Guy
when he gets back from the bank, shall we? He'll be
home soon.'

She swung one leg out of the hammock chair and groaned. 'Help me up, there's a nice child. There are *some* disadvantages in producing an infant—I'm beginning to feel like a barrel.'

Anthea stood up and held out both her hands. As she heaved Pamela to her feet, she said, 'Pam, have you told Nancy about me—you know, about losing the stuff in the fire and all that?'

'No, love. I didn't think you'd want it spread around.'

They walked arm in arm together towards the condo building. 'Thanks, that was tactful,' Anthea said. 'I don't want anyone but you and Guy to know. And I want to forget all about it for the time I'm here.'

Pamela nodded emphatically. 'Very sensible. We'll make sure you do.'

'Welcome to the Coconut Tree.' Pamela led Anthea into the restaurant later that evening. 'Romantic, don't you think?'

Guy had gone ahead to enquire about the table booked by his friend Bill. He came back to the two girls now. 'They haven't arrived yet, but our table's on the deck outside. Will that do for you, sweetheart? You wouldn't rather be inside?' He put a protective arm round his wife's waist, which was already starting to swell, and bestowed a frankly adoring look on her.

'Perfect for me!' Pamela returned the look with her beautiful limpid smile.

Watching the two of them, Anthea thought that they made the best argument she knew for the married state. More than five years and they were as much in love as ever.

Guy turned to her, quirking an eyebrow. 'I'm honoured to be escorting the two most beautiful ladies in the room.' He sketched a little bow.

Pamela chuckled as they followed him to where a waiter stood, indicating their table. 'Isn't Guy beautifully old-fashioned? He says such lovely things—and really means them.'

'Guy's a dear,' Anthea said, watching the back of her tall, upright brother-in-law in his rather formal attire of black trousers and white shirt. His fair hair was neatly brushed, and he walked with a stride that seemed to indicate that he was at home in the world and pleased with his place in it. 'And he's right about you anyway, Pam. You look gorgeous in that caftan.'

Pamela swished the folds of the loose, flowery garment. 'So useful when one's size is increasing daily! They're made locally and they have a huge selection in one of the shops in George Town. You'll have to indulge in one while you're here. But, to return the compliment, you look pretty good yourself, Thea, love. Is that top one of your own designs? I love the colours—the blue and green and the silver threads running through.'

Anthea nodded. 'Designed and made by my own fair hand—just before tragedy struck.' She tried to sound wry and jokey about it but it wasn't easy. 'I don't usually wear things I've made myself, but this had a small error in the pattern and I couldn't put it into stock. Lucky really, or it would have gone the way of all the rest—up in smoke.'

Pamela squeezed her arm in silent sympathy as they caught up with Guy and were installed at their table by a smiling dark-skinned waiter.

Anthea looked round and sighed with pleasure. If anything could heal the nasty wounds which had come her way recently, this holiday must surely be it. The evening was deliciously warm and the smell of succulent seafood mingled with that of the tall palm trees that overhung the sides of the deck. Almost immediately below, a line of white waves broke lazily on the sand, and beyond lay the darkness of the ocean under a black sky thick with stars. A white-suited quintet was playing Caribbean music on a dais in the corner, behind a bank of crimson and yellow flowers set among trailing greenery.

The tables round the central dance-floor were beginning to fill up, one or two couples were already dancing enthusiastically, and there was an atmosphere of laughter and light-hearted chatter. Anthea sat back, feeling relaxed and happy for the first time for weeks. Oh, yes, she could put her woes behind her and enjoy her stay here.

The waiter was hovering. Guy ordered drinks and said they would wait until their friends arrived to give the main order.

'Here they are now.' Pamela raised an arm in greeting. 'Trust Nancy to be punctual! And—oh, my goodness!'

'What?' enquired Guy, lifting his head from the menu.

Pamela gave a stifled laugh. 'Just—some baby brother!'

Anthea looked round to where Nancy Jamieson, in a blue and white candy-striped dress, was coming towards them across the wide deck. Beside her, her husband was short and spare, with thinning sandy hair

and gold-rimmed glasses. And behind them walked
the man who had to be Nancy's 'baby brother'.

Anthea felt her mouth go dry and her stomach
clench uncomfortably. She had the strangest feeling
that somewhere at the very back of her mind she had
known all the time that it would be Charles. He must
have decided to come on a later plane from Miami.

She watched him stride across the deck, and it
seemed as if he was walking straight towards *her*. She
almost expected him to come up and greet her. She
felt a smile of welcome begin to stretch her mouth—
the kind of smile you give to a friend you've known
for years.

The little group had reached the table now. 'Sorry
we're a bit late,' Nancy was saying in her blithe way.
'Pamela, do you know my brother, Charles
Ravenscroft? I think he came to your wedding party
with us, but I can't quite remember.'

Pamela laughed her silvery laugh. 'I can't remember a thing about it. Isn't it a shame? Your
wedding-day is supposed to be the greatest day of your
life, and you're so nervous that afterwards it's all a
blur! Hello, Charles——' she held out her hand
'—nice to meet you now, anyway. I'm sure you know
Guy, don't you? Nancy said you're a City chap. And
this is my young sister, Anthea.'

Anthea's smile had become fixed. Her hand went
out automatically. 'Hello,' she murmured. It was
absurd, this feeling of tension. What did she expect?
Of course he wouldn't remember her; he had probably
never seen her face clearly that night on the balcony—
and after the glamorous girl in white had appeared
he wouldn't have looked at *her*, even though he'd been
courteous enough to offer to finish their dance.

His hand touched hers briefly. 'Hello,' he said. His glance passed over her without recognition or interest—just as it had done in the airport lounge.

He turned to his sister. 'Where do you want me to sit, Nan?' He couldn't have made it plainer—short of absolute rudeness—that he didn't in the least want to be here.

Nancy introduced her husband Bill to Anthea, and then she fussed round, organising the seating. 'No, Pamela—Guy's going to entertain *me* tonight, aren't you, Guy?' She fluttered her eyelashes under the straight, dark fringe, mock-flirtatious. 'And Bill, you can practise your charm on Pamela. Anthea, you sit here—so that you can look out at the ocean. And Charles next to you.'

When Nancy had got them all settled to her satisfaction, drinks had been brought to the table, and the ordering had been done, Bill Jamieson said jovially, 'Well, this is very pleasant—our little party has expanded delightfully.' He raised his glass. 'Here's wishing you a super holiday, Anthea. And Charles too, of course.'

'Thank you,' Anthea said. Her throat was stiff and her mouth was dry, and she was ridiculously conscious of the man sitting next to her, dark and silent. This wouldn't do at all, she berated herself. She wasn't a teenager any longer, having love-sick fantasies about a marvellous man whose photograph was pinned up on her bedroom wall. She would be cool and poised, reminding herself that she had been the owner of a successful business until fate had stepped in and spoiled it.

The obvious thing to do was to remind him that they had met before. Put the situation on a casual

footing, where it belonged. She turned towards him.
'Didn't we meet five years ago at Pamela's wedding?
I seem to remember...'

She took a quick glance up at his dark, grim face.
The change in him from the man she remembered was
shocking. The mouth was drawn into bitter lines, the
dark eyes sombre, hooded, faintly bored. But, most
important of all, although it didn't show overtly, she
sensed a deep, corrosive anger.

He took a long swig of wine and reached for the
bottle to refill his glass, even before the waiter could
do it for him. 'Did we?' he said laconically. He turned
his head the merest fraction. 'I'm afraid my memory
doesn't go back as far as that,' he drawled.

If he had intended a snub then he could hardly have
done better. Anthea felt as if she'd been punched in
the stomach. Certainly she wasn't going to remind
him, with chapter and verse, of their brief earlier
meeting, and risk being snubbed again. Neither was
she going to submit tamely to such a deliberate put-
down.

Her eyes narrowed. Her soft lips curled. 'Mr Darcy,
I presume?' She had to take for granted that he was
familiar with Jane Austen's haughty, arrogant hero
in *Pride and Prejudice*.

Of course he was. From the corner of her eye she
saw him blink and jerk his head towards her, lips
parted, as if she had touched a sensitive nerve.

Too late, my friend, she thought with a small sense
of triumph, and smiled at Bill Jamieson, sitting on
her other side. 'Do tell me all about your new as-
signment,' she said sweetly. 'Are you both looking
forward to your stay in this paradise island?'

Bill Jamieson's eyes twinkled behind their gold-rimmed glasses. 'I hear good reports of it,' he said. 'It seems to be famous for two things—money and diving, in that order. I understand that there are more than three hundred wrecks to be investigated around the coast. And there are certainly more than three hundred banks here!'

Everyone laughed—except, of course, Charles Ravenscroft, who looked incapable of laughter, Anthea noted. The talk became general. Guy and Pamela were both eager to quiz their friends about London and all that was going on there. 'We'll feel like country cousins when we get back,' Pamela declared.

Bill and Guy had lots to talk about, mostly bank gossip. Nancy was anxious to have Pamela's tips about getting the best out of the shops in Grand Cayman. She was careful to include Anthea in the conversation—with a smile or a remark. Charles, for his part, lapsed into silence, eating very little of the succulent seafood dish that was served to them, and drinking freely of the fruity white wine.

As coffee was served, the jangling beat of the music changed to a slow rhythm. Guy took his wife's hand. 'Come on, sweetheart, this is something you can tackle if we take it gently.'

Pamela agreed with a laugh, and they moved on to the dance-floor. Nancy and Bill followed, Nancy opening her eyes wide in an encouraging backward glance towards her brother as they went.

Charles was left with the choice of being abominably rude—or asking Anthea to dance. For a moment or two they sat there together. Like a couple of waxworks, Anthea thought, and had a job to stop herself giggling.

You couldn't take Charles seriously, and she wasn't going to. She looked straight ahead of her and murmured, 'As I remember, Mr Darcy didn't consider any of the ladies worthy to lead on to the dance-floor. No doubt you wish to continue acting in character.'

He grunted angrily, 'I don't like being needled.' There was a silence. And then he growled roughly, 'Do you want to dance?'

'I always want to dance,' she said brightly, 'if my partner is up to my standard, *and* if I'm asked courteously.'

He got to his feet, frowning, and gripped her wrist, almost pushing her past the tables and on to the dance-floor. Both his arms went round her waist, pulling her hard against him as if he wanted to punish her—and perhaps he did. There was nowhere for her own arms to go but round his neck, and she put them there.

He was a superb dancer—as she remembered well. They moved as one person, her steps following his effortlessly. He might be behaving disgustingly but at least he couldn't change the way he moved his body—rhythmically, subtly, fitting them both to the languorous beat of the music.

Dancing under the stars! Anthea thought dreamily. Oh, it was wonderful! She could go on like this forever! Her head reached to his chin and she laid it against the thin stuff of his shirt, feeling the warmth from him spreading all over her, revelling in the dangerous *frissons* of delight that ran along her nerves.

He drew her even closer, and suddenly she was aware that he was aroused. Anger did that to a man, didn't it? she thought dizzily, and he was very, very angry. Should she draw away prudishly?

She found she was totally unable to move out of his close embrace. It was shaming the way she felt waves of sheer lust rippling in her stomach. Her arms tightened round his neck, and she knew that if they'd been alone in some solitary place she would have invited his kisses—and much, much more.

The music stopped. For a moment longer he held her; then he drew away and, with a hand at the small of her back, guided her towards their table.

The other two couples were coming back, laughing and talking. Anthea caught Pamela's eyes dancing mischievously and saw the message in them. Well done, Thea, she seemed to be saying. Carry on with the good work!

They sat down, and Charles reached for the bottle of wine and filled his glass. He drained it at a gulp, and sat frowning straight ahead of him. Just as Anthea was making herself believe that she had imagined what had just taken place between them, he turned to her and rapped out, 'I'm trying to remember. Did we really meet at that wedding party?'

It was fiendishly difficult to meet his eyes with a cool, slightly puzzled look, but somehow she managed it. At all costs she mustn't let him guess how that dance had disturbed her. 'Oh—that! I'm not sure, really. At first I thought I remembered you, but there were so many people there. I might have been mistaken.'

Guy and Pamela were getting ready to leave, and she got to her feet. Guy said, 'Pamela needs her early nights, but you stay on by all means, Anthea, if you like. Bill will drive you back.'

'Oh, no, thanks,' she said hastily. 'I'll come along with you. I need an early night too. I'm not quite over my jet lag yet.'

Nancy pulled a face. 'End of party! But I'm sure you're both right. We'll get along too, shall we, Bill? Are you ready, Charles?'

He shrugged. 'I'll walk back. Don't wait up for me. We'll settle up later for the dinner, Bill.' And, with a curt nod towards the party in general, he turned and walked away.

Nancy watched the tall form threading its way between the tables without a backward glance, and sighed. 'Poor old dear! He's taking it hard.'

Taking what hard? Anthea wondered. Had he lost a girlfriend—a mistress? A wife, perhaps? She wondered if Nancy had confided in Pamela. But whatever the circumstances it was quite unforgivable to behave as he had done. Boorish—rude—ill-mannered. Whatever had happened to the wonderful man she'd developed an adolescent crush on five years ago? He wouldn't be anyone's pin-up now. Or would he? She remembered with a little shiver how she'd felt when he'd held her in his arms on the dance-floor. Just sex, she told herself. And not particularly admirable with a man who was behaving like that. Forget it.

'Coming, Thea?' Suddenly she was aware that Guy and Pamela were waiting for her. Hastily she followed them out to the car.

It was a very short drive to the condo, where the two families had their apartments next door to each other. Their cars pulled up side by side in the car park.

They all agreed that it had been a delightful evening, and nobody mentioned Charles. Nancy said, 'We may as well make the most of our time before the doors of the bank close on poor Bill when he starts work properly. How about a four at tennis tomorrow morning? Us two against Charles and Anthea? And poor Pam can sit and cheer us on. You do play, don't you, Anthea?'

Pamela put in quickly, 'Anthea's first-class. Coming up to county standard.'

Anthea demurred. 'That was years ago. I haven't played for ages. I don't think I could...' She really didn't want to encounter Charles again so soon.

'Rubbish,' Pamela said briskly. 'Of course you could. What time, Nancy?'

It was arranged that they should meet on the court belonging to the condo complex at ten. 'Before it gets really hot,' Nancy added. 'Good—we'll look forward to it.'

In the apartment Guy announced that he had some work to do and settled down at his desk in the big living-room, a whisky beside him. Pamela planted a kiss on top of his head and said, 'Me for bed. You too, Thea? Let's brew up a cuppa and depart there, shall we?'

The kitchen was a dream: gleaming white, small and compact, with every up-to-the-minute gadget built in.

'I'll make the tea,' Anthea offered. 'Just show me where things are, then I can lend a hand while I'm here. It'll be a joy to work in a kitchen like this. You go and get into bed and I'll bring it up to you.'

Ten minutes later Pamela was installed in the big double bed, a froth of pale blue georgette round her shoulders, her golden hair loose around her face. As Anthea put the tray down on the bedside table and sank into a basket-chair near the bed, Pamela said rather too casually, 'Well, what did you think of the "baby brother"? Rather gorgeous, isn't he?'

'Looks count for very little,' said Anthea crisply, bending her head over the teapot, 'when their owner is such a double-dyed pain in the neck.'

Pamela chuckled. 'He did look rather grim, didn't he? Crossed in love, poor dear. I expect he'll perk up in a day or two. Good dancer, is he? I thought the two of you looked rather marvellous together.' She took the cup that Anthea handed her with a sideways glance.

'Oh, he can dance OK,' Anthea said with a shrug, glad of the shaded light as she felt a wave of heat surge into her cheeks.

She'd always confided in Pamela, but now she found to her surprise that she didn't want to talk to her about Charles, about how they had met at the wedding and what had happened. She snuggled back into her chair. 'Oh, isn't this *nice*? Being together—like old times! Now, I want to hear all about the baby. I can't wait to become an aunt. Have you decided what to call him—her?'

They drank their tea companionably, and the conversation, diverted into safe channels, lasted until Anthea began to yawn.

'Off to bed with you,' Pamela ordered. 'I'm taking you in hand, my girl. You need plenty of fresh air and sunshine and sleep. Juliana will bring your breakfast up in the morning—she's my household treasure. Comes in for a couple of hours each day, and is willing to oblige in the evening if required. Goodnight, love.' She held out her arms, and Anthea went into them and was soundly hugged.

She felt like a little girl again as she went off to her bedroom, taking the tea-tray to the kitchen on her way. As she undressed she thought about Pamela and how marvellous she had been when Mummy had died. Pamela had been sixteen and already a beauty, with her corn-gold hair and vivid blue eyes. She'd had dozens of boys after her, but she'd always found time for the heartbroken, ten-year-old Anthea, who, in turn, had adored her elder sister, clung to her, and turned to her for advice and comfort as she would have turned to her mother.

Pamela hadn't changed: still serene, still kind, still thinking the best of everyone and making excuses for them. Look how she'd jumped to make excuses for the utterly inexcusable conduct of Charles this evening.

Charles! But she didn't want to think about Charles. She *wouldn't* think about Charles. Charles had turned out to be the biggest disappointment of her life.

'Poor dear' Pamela had called him. Poor dear, indeed! Being crossed in love didn't have to make you an insufferable boor. She'd been crossed in love herself, hadn't she? But she wasn't taking it out on everyone around.

Anthea turned out the light and padded across to the window. What a magic place this was! The moon had just risen and was streaking the darkness of the ocean with silver. From here she could see over the tops of the casuarina trees right down to the beach.

And there, at the margin of the tide, she saw a tall figure walking slowly, head bent. Even from this distance, she knew it was Charles.

There was something forlorn about that solitary figure, and just for a second Anthea felt a tug of pity.

Then she whirled round and closed the curtains with a snap. Why should she pity the man, for heaven's sake? You couldn't feel sorry for someone who was so patently sorry for himself.

And yet it wasn't quite like that. She remembered sensing the anger buried deep inside him.

Oh, well, it hadn't anything to do with her, and the less she saw of Charles Ravenscroft the better. If she could get out of the tennis game tomorrow without being unfriendly to his pleasant sister Nancy, then she would. She'd come here for a quiet, restful holiday, not to be made the butt of a man with an outsized chip on his shoulder.

But, as she slid under the light silky duvet, she heaved a long sigh before she settled down to sleep. It felt like a kind of betrayal to discover that your idol had feet of clay.

CHAPTER THREE

ANTHEA awoke next morning to the sound of the curtains' being swished back and the sight of a dark-skinned girl with a scarlet bow in her black hair standing beside the bed, beaming down at her.

'Good morning, miss. I'm Juliana and I've brought your breakfast.' The soft voice had a faint lilt to it, and the smile was delightfully friendly.

Anthea pulled herself up in the bed and smiled back. 'Hello, Juliana. Well, this *is* a treat,' she said, as the girl deposited a breakfast-tray upon her knees. 'I don't have anyone back at home to bring me breakfast in bed. It looks delicious.' She gazed with unashamed greed at the crisp rolls and butter, the preserves in little crystal dishes. A ripe peach reposed on another dish and a silver pot of coffee wafted its fragrance over the room.

Juliana nodded enthusiastically, and the red bow bobbed up and down. 'Enjoy your meal.' With the standard pleasantry, she smiled again and departed.

Anthea certainly did enjoy her meal, but she didn't linger over it. There was something she had to arrange with Pamela as soon as possible.

She showered, pulled a thin wrap over her panties and bra, brushed her silky light-brown hair and went looking for her sister. The sound of a vacuum cleaner led her to the long, sunny living-room, where Juliana told her that the master had had breakfast and left for the bank, and the missus was still in bed.

38

Master...missus—how delightfully old-fashioned, Anthea thought, tapping at the bedroom door.

'Come in, Thea. Good morning. I'm being lazy.' Pamela put down a copy of *The Times* on the bed. 'One good thing about living out of the world is that when you read all the bad news it's out of date and much too late to start worrying about. How are you, love? Sleep well?'

'Marvellously. And I've had a super breakfast. I like your treasure Juliana; she's a sweetie.'

'Yes, isn't she? The islanders are the nicest people; I've always got on very well with them.'

Pamela would get on very well with anybody. She just wanted everyone to be happy and did her best to see that it happened. Which made it rather difficult for Anthea to say what she had come to say.

She perched on the bottom of the bed. 'About this game of tennis...' she began doubtfully.

'Yes, it was a brainwave of Nancy's to suggest it. Nothing like some hard exercise to chase away the blues. Billy and Nancy are a good pair—I've seen them play—and you and the "baby brother" should team up well together.' The blue eyes glinted with mischief. 'I've got a suspicion that Nancy's putting great store by you as a healer of hearts, Thea, love.'

This had to stop—*now*. Anthea could almost see a trap closing on her. And she was sure that Charles wouldn't want to be in the trap any more than she did. 'Look, Pam,' she began firmly, 'I'm really not keen on being a healer of hearts. I wasn't at all impressed with the man last night; in fact I thought he was absolutely the end—so rude and aloof. He made no effort to hide the fact that he didn't want to be with us.'

Pamela reached out and touched Anthea's hand. 'Oh, I don't think he really meant it, love. He was just in a bad mood. You have to make allowances.'

'Do you? Well, I'm not sure I want to. And I certainly don't want to partner him at tennis. Anyway, I haven't got a tennis dress with me.'

'A bikini?'

'Not on your life!' The thought of Charles Ravenscroft's insolent gaze passing over her near-naked body made the blood rush into her cheeks.

Pamela was laughing openly now. 'Goodness, the man *has* got under your skin, hasn't he?'

'I just hate his type,' Anthea said rather grumpily.

Pamela was easing herself out of bed. 'Well, give him another chance, there's a dear. Nancy would be so disappointed if you called it off. I've got a natty little tennis number you can wear.' She opened the wardrobe and flicked along the rail, selecting a mini-dress of white silky material, finely pleated, with pale blue hand-embroidery round the low neck. 'Here you are—this'll fit beautifully.' She pulled a wry face. 'Some day it may even fit me again. *And*——' she rummaged in a drawer and pulled out a pair of frilly white lace knickers '—here you are, centre court style! Now, get yourself ready, there's a dear, and we'll go down and meet the others.'

Anthea sighed and took the garments. 'Do you always get your own way?'

'Only when I'm right.' Pamela wrinkled her pretty nose and shooed her sister off.

In her own room Anthea slipped into the white dress and zipped it up the back. It was *extremely* short. She certainly couldn't wear it with the panties she had on.

Reluctantly she took them off and thrust her long, slim legs into the frilly knickers.

At home, when she'd had time to play tennis recently, she'd gone in for much more businesslike attire—usually shorts and a cotton shirt. This luxuriously expensive garb wasn't her style at all. She twisted before the long mirror, letting her silky brown hair flop against her neck. Yesterday's sunbathing session had turned her skin just a touch brown—about the colour of a rich tea biscuit, sufficient to contrast with the pure white of the dress. Not bad, she thought reluctantly, not bad at all. She looked more like Pamela than she had ever done before.

Ah, well, here I come—the healer of hearts. And I hope you're in a better temper this morning, Charles!

The two girls went down at ten o'clock to find Nancy alone outside the front entrance to the condo. 'Hello, good morning—isn't it a marvellous day?' she greeted them cheerfully. 'Charles went out for a stroll; he'll be back in a minute—ah, here he is now.'

Her brother sauntered up from the beach towards them, swinging a racket loosely in his left hand. Anthea could see at a glance that he wasn't relishing this game of tennis any more than she was herself. But she had to admit that he looked heart-stoppingly gorgeous in very brief navy shorts and a white knitted cotton vest. Working behind a desk in the City couldn't provide that healthy tan, those whipcord muscles in his legs and arms. But of course he could afford winter holidays in the sun, like this one.

'Good morning, Charles. Ready for the fray?' Pamela carolled.

He managed a grunted, 'Morning,' and then, flicking his racket against his heel and looking at nobody in particular, 'Shall we go, then?' He didn't actually add 'and get it over as quickly as possible', but he was quite obviously thinking it.

Nancy said, 'Afraid there's been a slight change of plans. Poor old Billy's just had a call from the bank and they want him in there this morning—something to do with his new office. He went off a few minutes ago—grumbling like mad. He said to offer his apologies, Anthea, and we'll have to put off the doubles until another day.'

'Oh, that's quite OK,' Anthea murmured, but she thought her words were drowned by Charles's brisk,

'Right! If I'm not wanted I'll get along to the dive-shop, then. Put this inside for me, Nan.' He held the racket out to her.

'Hey, steady on.' Nancy was laughing, but there was more than a touch of the elder sister in her voice. 'You and Anthea can have a set of singles. Go along, the two of you, and Pamela and I will come and watch in a few minutes.' She turned to Pamela. 'I found the magazine I was telling you about, Pamela—the one with the pattern for a dear little matinée jacket. I'd just love to knit it for you if you'd like it. Come along in and I'll show it to you.'

She linked her arm with Pamela's and led her back to the open door. 'Have a good game, you two,' she called over her shoulder.

Anthea almost followed them, but a small devil inside her made her stay where she was beside Charles, and say brightly, 'Shall we go, then? Will you show me where the court is?'

She made herself glance up at his face. He looked just as angry as he had done last evening when his sister had manoeuvred him on to the dance-floor.

'Do you really want to play tennis?' he said ungraciously.

Rude brute, Anthea thought; she wasn't going to let him get away with it. 'Of course,' she said, looking surprised. 'I thought that was your sister's suggestion.'

'Another of her little tricks,' he muttered under his breath. 'Come on, then.' He strode away at a great pace along the path, which led round the buildings to a green cement tennis court. There was a thatched hut at one end where pink bougainvillaea rioted. Low-growing trees around the court provided partial shade, and, here and there between the trees, glimpses of the sea flashed vivid blue in the sunshine.

'Isn't it a lovely day?' Anthea tossed out the social cliché in hope, but got no response whatever. Charles went into the hut and came out with a handful of balls, which he dumped on to the court. Then he felt in his pocket for a coin and tossed it. 'Heads,' said Anthea.

Heads it was. 'I'll take this side, you can serve,' she said, glancing doubtfully at him. Was the whole game to be played in an atmosphere of glacial silence?

He picked up a couple of balls and patted them across the net to her with a contemptuous flick of the wrist. She returned them without difficulty and realised that it wouldn't take long for her to get into form again. Charles probably played very well—she couldn't judge from the patronising way he was behaving—but she felt sure she could give him a game, allowing for the fact that a good man player would always beat a good woman player.

She went back to the baseline and tried a few services, while he stood looking bored.

She felt her temper surfacing. The man was insufferable. She gathered the loose balls together and sent them back to his end of the court. 'Go on, then—serve, if you've quite finished play-acting.' She glared at him fiercely and stalked back to the baseline.

When she turned to receive service and saw the anger in his face she had a moment of doubt. She remembered the steely note in his voice last evening when he had said, 'I don't like being needled.' Golly, she thought, now I've got under his skin.

There was a brief moment when he flung the ball high, coiling his body, and even from this distance she could see the power in the man, the tension under perfect control like a great steel spring.

Then he served.

It wasn't merely a hard service. It was a calculatedly vicious service. The ball that came scorching over the net straight at her might have been sent down by Becker to McEnroe at a critical moment in a Wimbledon final. As a service from a man to a girl in a friendly match it was quite unforgivably aggressive, even dangerous.

Some instinct of self-preservation made Anthea throw up her racket before her face. By a pure fluke the ball made contact—the force of it jerking her back on her heels—and dropped dead on the opposite side of the net. If she had intended to play the shot it would have ranked as a superb stop-volley.

The man at the other end of the court didn't move to return the shot. He stood quite still on the service-line and stared at the ball rolling across the green surface of the court, as if he couldn't believe what had happened.

There were two chairs beside the left-hand net-post. Furious, Anthea walked over and sat down on one of them, rubbing her palm, which was stinging from the impact of his shot, and uncomfortably aware that her legs were trembling. She couldn't have felt more upset if she'd been mugged.

That, of course, was the last game of tennis she would play with Mr Charles Ravenscroft. Short and—certainly not sweet.

After a time he came slowly across the court and sat down on the chair beside her in a heavy silence, elbows on knees, head bent.

Anthea edged as far away from him as possible. She was beginning to recover her cool now. 'You know, there must be better ways,' she said, her voice dripping with irony. 'You could try poisoning my wine, or pushing me over a cliff.'

He raised his head and the dark face was haggard. 'What can I say?'

She examined the strings of her racket. 'You might start by saying you're sorry. Then you might offer to have Pamela's racket restrung. The poor thing isn't quite up to your standard.'

He ran a hand through his dark hair. 'OK, I *am* sorry. It was bloody ill-mannered, boorish, crass. I really don't know...'

'What came over you? It was obvious—you wanted to murder someone. But, as you really don't know me at all, I can hardly think you intended me to be the victim. Or did you?' She looked at him with interest.

'Don't be ridiculous,' he muttered.

She leaned her chin on the top of the racket handle, and gazed thoughtfully at a brightly plumaged bird pecking in the grass under the trees. 'It may not be so ridiculous. I have a suspicion that your sister Nancy is doing her best to foist me off on you as a holiday playmate, and that the idea is—to put it politely—unacceptable to you. You've made that quite clear from the start, as the politicians say. Well, for your information, *my* sister seems to have the same idea, and it doesn't appeal to me any more than it appeals to you.'

'It doesn't?' He sounded genuinely surprised.

'No, it certainly doesn't. You're the last person I'd want to spend my time with. So, now we both know where we stand, we shall know what to do about it.' She stood up and turned away from him.

'Hang on a bit.' His hand shot out and gripped her wrist, and Anthea came to a sudden stop. His touch was hard and dry, and the sensation that ran up her arm was quite unmistakable. Sexual magnetism, she thought; that's all it is. Well, she knew the man was magnetic, didn't she? You've only got to look at him. Ignore it.

'Sit down,' he rapped out, and she found herself obeying. Not, of course, because he had told her to, but because she was mildly interested to hear what he had to say.

'You're quite right,' he said. 'My sister has this pathetic idea that because she has a satisfactory marriage herself it's possible and desirable for everyone else to have one. Recently, since my—since a relationship came to an end, Nancy has been producing a string of nubile young girls to tempt my appetite and mend my broken heart.' His voice was hatefully cynical. 'I'm afraid it always works in reverse. I'm just not prepared to get involved. So I must warn you straight away, Miss—er—Anthea. At the risk of being ill-mannered once again, I must tell you that, as far as I'm concerned, there's nothing doing.'

Anthea turned her head slowly towards him, her eyes widening in disbelief. Then she burst into uncontrollable laughter.

'Am I funny?' he demanded, outraged.

'No, not funny,' she choked. 'Just disgustingly pompous. Didn't you hear what I said—that I don't relish your company?' She regarded the scowling black brows with mild interest. 'Are you always like this? Isn't it rather tiring to keep yourself in such a beastly mood all the time?'

He shot her a nasty look. 'What are you trying to do, Little Miss Sunshine? Can't you understand that there are times in a man's life when it's bloody irritating to be cheered up?'

'Quite,' she said crisply, and stood up again. 'Now, if you'll excuse me——'

He was on his feet too, barring her way. 'I thought we were supposed to be playing tennis. We'll be in the doghouse with our respective sisters if they don't find us here, enjoying ourselves. I've apologised for my earlier lapse and I promise it won't happen again, so what about it?'

She looked up uncertainly and thought she caught the merest gleam of amusement in the liquid dark eyes, but of course she might have been mistaken.

To her intense annoyance her own eyes refused to hold his and she looked away in confusion. 'Very well,' she said stiffly and marched back to her end of the court. 'Your service, wasn't it?'

After what had happened, she half expected him to put on a patronising show of pat-ball. Instead he

sent down a medium-paced service which she returned without difficulty. A brisk rally followed,
lasting until Anthea managed to finish it with an ac-
curate backhand drive.

Charles was smiling grimly when he came up to the
net to retrieve a loose ball. 'It's like that, is it? OK,
we'll see.'

She'd surprised him. She'd even made him smile—
well, sort of smile. It was quite amazing what a
pleasant glow that gave her as she walked back to receive his next service.

Anthea loved tennis, and what followed was quite
the most exciting game she had ever played. She was
out of practice, but for some reason the sight of the
tall figure of the man on the other side of the net
challenged her to lift her game, and quite soon she
found herself flying around the court, driving and
volleying and smashing, just the way she had done
when she'd played in the first team at college.

Charles paid her the compliment of giving her no
quarter, except that he kept his enormous strength in
leash.

He won the set, of course, but Anthea was delighted to have taken three games from him, and, when
she finally collapsed on to the seat at the side of the
court, she was breathing hard and feeling fitter than
she'd done for weeks past.

She said, 'I enjoyed that.'

He didn't sit down beside her. 'You play very well,'
he said formally.

He stood looking down at her, frowning slightly,
as if there was something he was trying to say. And
suddenly she saw how five years had aged him. There

were deep lines on his wide forehead, dark hollows
under his eyes, and his face was thinner.

He went on staring at her. All the anger had drained
out of him, perhaps with the physical effort of the
game, and she saw a deep sadness in his face. 'I
wish...' he muttered. He touched her shoulder briefly.
'I didn't mean to be so foul to you ... I ...' He gave
a start and drew himself up. 'I must go,' he said in
quite a different tone. 'Perhaps you'll excuse me?'

She watched him walk away, racket under his arm,
dark head bent, the sunshine turning his strong arms
and legs to deep gold. When he reached the thatched
hut he stopped and looked back over his shoulder,
and she saw that he was still frowning. Then he walked
round the side of the hut and was gone.

Anthea stared at the place where he had disappeared from view, her eyes widening. In those last
few moments she had seen the Charles she remembered. She almost expected him to come back, smiling
that slow, sleepy smile that she had thrilled to every
time she'd stood adoring the Charles of her pin-up
photograph.

Then, very slowly, the little thatched hut smothered
in bougainvillaea turned upside down and floated
before her eyes in a smudgy haze of pink before it
righted itself again even more slowly. Her insides
began to churn with an almost painful sensuousness.
She sagged back against the hard wooden rail of the
seat and closed her eyes.

Something earth-shaking and utterly appalling had
just become clear to her. The old magnetic attraction
that she had felt five years ago for this man was still
as strong as ever.

She touched her shoulder where his hand had rested, and a wave of love and compassion shook her to the depths of her being. He had been terribly hurt and she wanted quite desperately to comfort him. She felt a violent hate for the woman who had had the power to change him into the bitter, cynical man he was now.

She had no idea how long she sat there. It might have been minutes or hours. But then she was vaguely conscious of a voice coming from somewhere behind her.

'Hi there!' it said. 'Are you OK?'

Anthea blinked towards the place the voice had come from, and was hazily aware of a very tall, lanky young man pushing aside an overlap in the stop-netting just behind her.

'Sorry if I woke you up. Mind if I join you?' He sat down beside her. 'Peter Jordan,' he introduced himself. 'Looking for a quiet game of tennis. Have I struck lucky, Miss...?'

Anthea stared at him stupidly. 'Lloyd,' she murmured. 'Anthea Lloyd.'

'How about it, then, Anthea? Will you give me a game?'

She stared at him blankly—he might have been a stranger from another planet. She dragged herself back from a distant place where she had been floating in a dream about Charles confiding in her, telling her that what he needed was a girl who understood him and truly loved him.

'A game...?' she muttered vaguely.

This was ridiculous—she *must* pull herself together. She gave herself a little shake, aware that the young man was waiting for her answer. Forcing herself to concentrate on him, she saw that he had floppy, non-

descript hair, and was wearing jazzy Bermuda shorts
and a T-shirt with a lobster on the front. She murmured, 'I'm sorry, I must have dozed off—I'm not
quite awake yet.'

'I promise to lose if you play with me,' he said
cheerfully. 'I make a habit of it. I'm not very good,'
he added with humorous resignation.

'Oh, I'm sure you are,' she murmured. What was
he talking about?

'I'm not—scout's honour! You're looking at the
world's worst sportsman, the one who's crazy about
sport. Tennis, golf, football, marbles, shove ha'penny,
tiddly-winks, kiss-in-the-ring—I love 'em all and I'm
a no-hoper at every one. Except the last one, maybe.'
He slid her a meaningful glance.

Oh, lord, not that! The last thing she needed was
to be landed with a flirtatious young man. She got to
her feet, and just then she caught a glint of red out
of the corner of her eye and turned to see Nancy
coming towards them from the direction of the hut.
Even from this distance, the bewildered dismay on
her face was obvious.

'Where's Charles?' she hissed as she got near
enough.

Anthea joined her, doing her best to appear un-
concerned. 'He went off somewhere; he didn't say
where he was going.'

'Oh, that's too bad of him,' his sister said crossly.
'He really is the limit—I'm so sorry, Anthea.'

'It didn't matter a bit,' Anthea lied. 'Do you two
know each other?' she asked, as Peter Jordan came
up beside her.

But Nancy didn't stay to chat. 'I'll see where Charles
has got to,' she said, biting her lip in annoyance, and

strode off, her scarlet sun-dress slapping against her ample thighs.

Anthea turned in the opposite direction, murmuring an excuse about being too hot to play. She *had* to get away by herself.

But Peter Jordan wasn't to be dismissed so easily. He walked beside her, chatting brightly. To Anthea it sounded like a radio that wasn't quite tuned in, a voice going on and on. '...arrived last week...holiday with the parents...something in the bank in London...a flat in Hampstead with two other guys...

'How about you, Anthea?' he shot at her suddenly.

'Me?' She blinked. She'd only taken in about a quarter of what he'd been saying. 'Oh, I'm staying with my sister Pamela and my brother-in-law.'

'Guy Stokes-Neville? Yes, I know them. Guy works with my dad. Pamela's a real beauty, isn't she?' He cast a frankly admiring glance down at her. 'It runs in the family, of course.'

They had arrived at the pool-side by now. Pamela was lying in a green recliner, a huge straw hat pulled forward to shade her eyes. If she was surprised to see Anthea appearing with Peter Jordan instead of Charles, she didn't show it. 'Hello, you two. I'm being lazy. Have you been energetic enough to play tennis?'

'Hello, Mrs Stokes-Neville.' Peter's tone was just a touch deferential. He had nice manners—not like some, Anthea thought darkly. 'Anthea found it rather too hot for a game—which she certainly would have won,' he added wryly.

'Poor Peter!' Pamela gave him her creamy smile. 'Never mind, you'll start winning all before you one day.' She evidently knew about Peter's avowed hopelessness at games.

There was a squeal of, 'Peter!' from the far end of the pool, where several sun-bronzed bodies were disporting themselves, and a curvaceous girl approached at a fast crawl and hung on to the side. 'Pete—come along in! I'm waiting to win against you over five lengths.' Tendrils of wet red hair were plastered becomingly over an attractive small face, and two perfect rows of white teeth glistened in the sunshine as the girl laughed up at him invitingly.

Peter grimaced comically at Anthea. 'You see? I'm always relied on to lose. OK, Babs, be with you in a jiffy.' He loped off towards the condo.

Pamela looked up at Anthea curiously. 'What goes? Nancy went off to watch you and Charles playing tennis.'

'She was much too late.' Anthea rummaged in her beach-bag for her dark glasses. 'The set was over very quickly. Charles slaughtered me.'

Pamela patted the empty chair beside her. 'Come and relax, then, and get over it.'

Anthea stepped backwards hastily. 'No, I—I think I'll go in. I'm just longing for a shower.'

'Why not put on a swim-suit and dive in the pool?' Pamela suggested.

'I—I'd rather go inside,' Anthea said lamely. 'It's a bit too hot for me out here.'

Her sister sat up, regarding her anxiously. 'You're OK, love? You haven't overdone it on your first day?'

'I'm fine—fine. Just hot. See you later,' she murmured, and escaped across the grass. She felt confused and upset, and she needed time to think before she encountered Pam's questioning gaze again.

Upstairs in her room, she sank into a chair beside the big open window. The sun was warm on her arms and legs. A breeze bearing a delicate scent of flowers touched her cheeks. The sound of shrieks and splashes came from the pool as if from a long, long way away.

She'd been shocked by the sudden strength of her feelings out there on the tennis court. Didn't they say that pity was akin to love? And Charles had looked so desperately unhappy. She had had a wild desire to stroke his dark hair—to comfort him. She had had to stop herself from jumping up and running after him.

What idiocy! she thought now. She could well imagine the scathing look he would have given her.

She'd be completely crazy to start mooning over a man who had showed plainly that he didn't want her company. Even his slight apology had seemed to be dragged out of him.

And as for finding the Charles she remembered underneath the armour of cynicism and bitterness— what hope was there of that? She wasn't the kind of girl who could 'foist herself', as he had so elegantly described it, on a man who didn't want her. Let him go off on his own and brood if that was what he wanted. *She* was going to enjoy her holiday on this paradise island.

Goodness only knew what she was going to find waiting for her when she got back to London; it wasn't going to be easy to start all over again. So she must be bounding with health and high spirits and ready to tackle anything. She certainly mustn't return as a pale and pathetic lovelorn creature.

She didn't even have to decide to keep away from Charles. He had shown quite plainly that he wanted to keep away from her. So that made everything much simpler, didn't it?

Before she could find any flaws in this sensible conclusion, she got up and showered, changed into a cheerful yellow sun-dress, and went down to have lunch with Pamela.

CHAPTER FOUR

'WHAT is it between you and Charles Ravenscroft?' Pamela's lovely face was alive with curiosity as she pushed a cup of coffee across the table to Anthea. 'There's *something*, I can tell. You looked positively shattered when you came along with Peter Jordan. Don't tell me you'd had words with Charles. You haven't taken an instant dislike to the man, have you?'

The sisters were lunching together in the long, cool living-room, shaded by the canopy that covered the veranda outside, where bunches of green grapes hung from the slatted-wood roof.

It was just as well, Anthea thought, that she was ready for Pamela's good-natured quizzing. She said wryly, '*He* seems to have taken an instant dislike to *me*.' That was near enough to the truth to put Pamela off the scent.

'Hm, it didn't look like that when you were dancing together last night.' Pamela sighed gustily. 'He's so gorgeous, isn't he? And you looked so lovely together.'

Anthea concentrated on peeling a ripe pear. 'Pam, dear, don't start imagining things. And don't try to pair me off with Charles Ravenscroft. I'm sure he isn't in a mood just now to be paired off with anyone— which really couldn't concern me less.'

She felt a twinge of guilt. In the old days she had always confided anything and everything to Pamela— had never had any secrets from her. But the idea of opening her heart to anyone about Charles filled her with a kind of panic.

Pamela said thoughtfully, 'His sister Nancy absolutely idolises him. She's talked to me about him for hours—how kind he is, how generous, what fun he can be.'

'Hmm,' put in Anthea with dark scepticism.

'And he must have a very good brain,' Pamela went on imperturbably. 'He and a friend have built up a successful financial business in London, and it's going from strength to strength, Nancy says.' Pamela turned her limpid blue eyes on Anthea. 'You don't want to judge him too quickly, love. Most men act up one way or another after a break-up with a girl. He's just taken it badly, that's all—he'll get over it. I'm sure if you got to know him better——'

'Pamela!' Anthea laughed shakily. 'Stop it this minute. It's clear that Charles isn't interested in girls just now. In fact, I think he's trying to get away on his own.'

'Mmm, well, it looks as if he wasn't trying quite hard enough,' Pamela said. 'Look at that.'

Through the window Anthea saw the tall figure of Charles striding along the path from the beach. He had taken off his shirt and looped it over his arm, and his broad chest glistened in the sunlight, the muscles rippling with health. Beside him, her arm linked with his, was the girl who had hailed Peter in the swimming pool—Babs, he'd called her. Her hair had dried into a fiery, frizzy cloud round her piquant little face, and her kelly-green bikini barely covered any of her slim brown body. She was laughing up into Charles's face, nestling close to him, and he was bending his dark head down to hers. They looked like a man and a girl revelling in the holiday atmosphere together.

Anthea felt jealous, as though a thin steel blade were piercing through her, and for a moment she thought she was going to be sick. She pressed a hand against her stomach, leaning forward so that Pamela wouldn't notice.

But Pamela was gazing out of the window with interest. 'It's Barbara Raikes—her father's manager of one of the big international companies with an office in George Town. She's been here for a week or so—I think she's a student at one of the American colleges. She's been going around with Peter Jordan. She's rather stunning, don't you think?'

Anthea swallowed hard. She said, 'Yes—very. I expect she's Charles's type. Now don't let's talk any more about him. I want to hear about you—all about the baby and everything . . .'

Her sister needed no encouragement, and Anthea drew a breath of relief. She had managed to get through that bad moment rather well, she congratulated herself. Seeing Charles unexpectedly like that— and with another girl—had given her a sharp twinge, but of course it was bound to happen in a place like this, so full of pretty girls. Next time it would be easier.

After lunch Pamela announced that she was going up to her room. She had to rest most of the afternoon, she told Anthea. 'I don't mind; I find I'm being delightfully lazy at this stage. Probably when Junior arrives I'll be made to pay for it. Sleepless nights— isn't that the price for having a baby?' She didn't look at all apprehensive.

Anthea gave her an affectionate glance. 'If he—she—inherits your temperament, Sis, I don't think you need worry. You must have been a really placid baby.'

'Mummy always said I wasn't any trouble.' Pamela's beautiful eyes clouded. 'Isn't it a shame she had to die? She was such a lovely person, and it would have been such fun to have had her with us still.' She was silent for a moment, then she said, 'How's it going with Janice? Do you see much of Daddy—and her?'

'Not more than I can help,' Anthea told her wryly. 'I rang Daddy to tell him about the fire. He said he was sorry, but I don't think it meant much to him. We're miles apart really. Janice invited me for Christmas, not very enthusiastically, but I declined with thanks. I thought—then—that I'd be spending Christmas with Geoffrey.'

Pamela said gently, 'You poor child—you've had to go through all this on your own. You know, you really *do* need a nice, kind, understanding husband.' She was only half joking.

Anthea held up a hand, laughing. 'No more of that—I value my independence. Now, off with you to have your rest.'

When Pamela had departed Anthea searched the bookcase, found a mystery novel she hadn't read and stretched out in a hammock chair on the veranda.

She had discovered some time ago that giving herself suggestions went some way to stopping worries scurrying round her brain like ants. Now she opened her book and muttered, 'You are *not* going to start thinking about Charles and that girl. You are not going to think about Charles at all—it would be a complete waste of your holiday time. You are going to read your book and get involved in the plot...'

Fortunately it was a mystery that had the quality of gripping from the very first paragraph. After an hour she was deep in chapter three and already making a shrewd guess about the identity of the murderer.

'Hello there—not asleep again, are you?' Peter Jordan's light voice roused her from her concentration.

She lifted her head as he came towards her across the veranda, looking fresh and groomed in white shorts and a sleeveless blue vest. 'No, wide awake.' She smiled at him, thinking he was a perfect example of the boy next door. So very different from Charles and his dark-eyed, sultry sophistication. 'Tracking down a murderer,' she added hastily. Why couldn't she put that man out of her mind?

Peter came nearer and glanced at the title of her book. 'Ruth Rendell—my favourite. I read that one last week. The wife of the garage man——'

'Don't tell me!' Anthea squealed in alarm. Peter was a nice boy but sadly lacking in subtlety.

'Sorry!' His fair cheeks flushed. 'I'm always putting my big foot in it.'

'Rubbish, of course you're not.' Anthea felt rather sorry for him. 'Where are you off to?' she asked him brightly.

'Going for a dive,' he told her. 'I had a lesson yesterday and it's grabbed me. The underwater scene is absolutely fabulous.' He eyed her shyly. 'Like to come along and have a go?'

Anthea hesitated. 'Is it difficult?'

'Dead easy,' he told her. 'I got the hang of it in no time at all. I'll teach you,' he added, confidence rising. 'You'll be safe with me, I promise. You can hire the gear at the dive-shop—that's what I did. How about it?' He grinned hopefully at her.

'What do I wear?' she said.

'Exactly what you're wearing.' He eyed her citrus-coloured bikini and the soft curves inside it with obvious admiration. 'You look smashing.'

Anthea got out of her chair, and marked the place in her book. 'I'll leave a note for Pamela, saying where I've gone.'

She went up to her bedroom, slipped on a green polyester-cotton dress over her bikini, picked up a towel and her handbag, and scribbled a note to Pamela, which she left on the table in the dining-room.

Then she joined Peter, and five minutes later they were bowling along the dusty road in his small hired car. 'There are lots of dive-shops in Grand Cayman,' he told her, 'some of them very pukka and attached to the big hotels. Joe's is one of the smaller ones but it's reckoned to be very good. He's well known to be an expert, no doubt about that.'

'Did he teach you?' Anthea enquired idly.

'Oh, no, he has several instructors working for him. I didn't even see him yesterday. As a beginner I didn't rate a lesson from the great man.' Peter grinned his deprecating grin. 'Here we are.'

The dive-shop was immediately behind and above the beach—a long wooden building with an open-air annexe beside it in the shade of the tall palm trees. The annexe obviously served as a coffee-bar and ice-cream parlour, and most of the white tables were occupied.

Anthea began to follow Peter into the shop, when a voice behind her said, 'Where are you off to?'

Her heart gave an uncomfortable jolt as she turned to see Charles behind her, not looking at all amiable.

'Peter's going to teach me to dive,' Anthea said sweetly. Peter had turned back and she sketched an introduction.

'Hi,' said Peter, holding out a large paw.

The handclasp was very brief. 'You have an instructor's certificate, of course?' Charles said brusquely.

Charles must be over six feet tall, Anthea thought, and Peter topped that by three or four inches; but he was only about half the width across the shoulders. They made an odd-looking pair as they stood eyeing each other suspiciously.

'Instructor's certificate? Well, no,' Peter said. 'We're only going cruising around. I had a lesson yesterday and I know the drill.' He seemed to stiffen his long backbone. 'What's it to do with you, anyway?' he demanded belligerently.

Charles's hooded glance raked the younger man from head to foot. 'If you're not qualified to teach a beginner you've no right to take Anthea out. I suggest you limit your activities to paddling in the shallows.'

Peter's fair cheeks were crimson. 'We'll see about that in the shop. Come on, Anthea, let's find out about hiring some gear for you.'

He marched into the dive-shop and Anthea, without another glance at Charles, followed him.

Inside there was a curious mixture of smells—wood and rubber and salt. Light coming in from a high window showed all the paraphernalia of diving. Anthea recognised some of it—the masks, the curved tubes, the fins. All these she had seen on TV, when

divers, surrounded by shoals of fish, glided effortlessly through the water or pried into beautiful coral
caves and wrecked ships.

Peter strode up to the counter, where a tough-
looking man, with skin burnt to a mahogany colour,
was reading a newspaper.

'Er—good afternoon,' Peter began. 'I hired some
gear yesterday afternoon and had a lesson—I don't
think I saw you.'

The man raised his head. 'No—I was out with the
boat.'

'I'd like to hire the same again, and for this young
lady too. I enjoyed it so much I'd like to get her
started.' His face was rather flushed, and Anthea
wondered if he was as confident as he sounded, or if
Charles's words had shaken him.

The man subjected Peter to the same scrutiny that
Charles had turned upon him. 'You're wanting an instructor? 'Fraid there's no one in just now.'

'Oh, I wasn't thinking of a lesson. I'm sure I picked
up enough to pass on my—er—expertise.' Peter
laughed a little self-consciously.

The man shook his head. 'Sorry, mate, we don't
hire diving gear to beginners going out alone. Too
dangerous.'

Peter looked as if he might be going to argue. 'I
only propose to keep this side of the reef...' he began,
but the man was still shaking his head.

A cool voice from behind them said, 'It's OK, Joe.
I'll go out with them.'

The man grinned over Anthea's shoulder. 'Hello,
Charlie; well—that's a different matter.' He prised
himself slowly out of his chair and strolled round the
counter, waving a rugged arm. 'Help yourself.'

Charles lounged across the cluttered shop towards a stand where face-masks hung from hooks. 'You look after the gentleman, Joe, and I'll fix the lady up. We'll stick to snorkelling for a start.'

Peter walked up to him, using his slightly superior height to make a show of looking down on Charles's dark head. 'Look here...' he began huffily.

Charles's eyes met his blandly. 'Yes?'

Peter hesitated—and was lost. 'Oh, have it your own way, then. You take Anthea out—I'll remove myself.' He turned. 'Sorry, Anthea.'

She had a horrid feeling that he was going to cry.

'No, don't go, Peter—I'll come with you,' she said. 'I'm not all that keen on diving. We could play tennis or—or something.' She felt desperately sorry for the young man. But Peter had turned and almost run out of the shop.

She took a couple of steps after him, but Charles's hand came out and closed over her arm. 'Let him go,' he said quietly. 'He'll get over it. We all have to learn.'

She glared at him. 'You needn't have been so—so quelling. You hurt his feelings badly—he's sensitive.' The dark eyes met hers and again she saw the bitterness in them.

'He isn't the only one,' he said flatly. Then, in a different tone, 'Now, how about having your first diving lesson? You may as well, now you're here. Joe has all the best gear in the island, haven't you, Joe?'

Joe grinned and lifted one thumb. 'If you say so, Charlie-boy.'

Anthea said coolly, 'May I take it that you have your instructor's certificate, Mr Ravenscroft?'

'As it happens, I have.'

The dark eyes glittered into hers as Joe guffawed loudly. 'He's the best, miss. You'll be safe with Charlie.'

Anthea was torn. She very much wanted to learn to dive and she didn't doubt that Charles would be an excellent teacher. If she accepted his offer it would seem like deferring tamely to his high-handed treatment of poor Peter. But her sense of fairness had to admit that he was probably right.

'Well? Made up your mind?' He was looming over her, thumbs stuck nonchalantly in the waistband of his navy shorts.

'Why do you want to waste your time teaching a beginner?' she said, looking out through the door to where a lesson was going on: several heads in masks were bobbing about in a small pool, their owners taking orders from a thin man—evidently an instructor.

'They're having a lesson out there,' she added. 'I could learn like that, couldn't I?'

'You could, of course. But it would be much quicker one to one. It's a straight offer—take it or leave it.'

Anthea had a short argument with her sensible self. It would be prudent to refuse. Dimly, she could sense danger ahead if she tangled with this man. But she did, very much, want to learn to dive.

'Well?' he asked impatiently.

'Thank you,' she said, 'I'd like to accept your offer.'

'Right!' he said matter-of-factly.

Suddenly Anthea had a mischievous urge to break through his aloofness. She slanted a glance up at him under her long curving lashes. 'That is,' she said, 'so long as it isn't your intention to drown me.'

He started as if she had struck him, his face as black as thunder. 'What the hell . . .?' Then, very gradually, his frown cleared. His long, sensitive mouth twitched at the corners, his lids lowered into the sleepy smile that Anthea remembered from five years ago.

'I . . . see. Well, I give you my word that your safety will be my first consideration,' he said with mock solemnity. 'Does that reassure you?'

His hand had closed on her upper arm as he'd led her towards the stands at the side of the shop. The touch of his fingers on her skin was doing strange things to her breathing. This man was dangerous to her peace of mind—she shouldn't be meekly agreeing to his invitation. She should be running away from him as fast as possible. Instead she heard herself saying, 'I'll hold you to that.'

She looked up into the dark sleepy eyes and they didn't move from hers. It seemed to her that the dive-shop with all its stacks of equipment faded away and there were just the two of them with an unspoken question hanging between them.

At last Charles shook his head puzzledly. 'I wish I could . . . Oh, well, never mind. Come along and I'll fit you with a mask. As I said, we'll stick to snorkelling for your first lesson. If you like we can progress to scuba later on.'

Anthea shook her head helplessly. 'Explain, please. I come from Birmingham—about as far away from the sea as you can get in England. I learned to swim on holidays in Cornwall when I was small, but diving is a closed book to me.'

'I see. Briefly, snorkelling is staying more or less on the surface of the water—although you can take brief trips downwards when you get confidence and if you're good at holding your breath. The mask is worn so that your eyes can work in their normal medium of air instead of underwater, and the snorkel tube allows you to breathe through it while swimming on the surface with your face submerged. Snorkelling is a good way of getting started. Once you experience the thrill of seeing what goes on underwater you very soon want to go deeper and deeper—which you can when you progress to scuba diving. That's when you carry your own supply of air in a cylinder on your back. Get the idea? Now, we'll fit you with a mask. It's very important to get a good fit so that it makes a proper seal against your face.'

Anthea had been watching Charles's face as he spoke, seeing how the strain and bitterness had ebbed away as he'd become engrossed in something that interested him.

Standing still while he selected a mask for her presented its own problems. His fingers, busy against her cheeks and pushing her hair away from her forehead, were sending little messages along her nerves. When he was finally satisfied he let his hand drift down to her neck and linger there long enough to make the gesture deliberate. His dark eyes, seen through the glass window in the mask, looked strangely intent.

'There,' he said. 'That feel comfortable?'

Anthea swallowed. It felt wonderful. Suddenly she ached for his hand to travel lower, to touch her body in all sorts of intimate places. 'Y-yes—fine,' she muttered.

'Good.' He removed the mask, speedy and businesslike again. 'This snorkel tube should do, and these fins. Just slip off your sandals and try them.'

Her knees felt curiously weak as she stood on her left foot to pull the sandal from the right one. She wobbled and reached to the counter nearby to steady herself. But Charles was there before her, a hand round her waist.

She pulled away with a jerk. 'I can manage, thanks.'

He removed his hand at once but she sensed, rather than saw, that he had noticed her reaction. Damn him, she thought, does he imagine I want to flirt with him? But I just hope he keeps his hands off me, because when he touches me I begin to melt.

She thrust her feet into the fins and he stooped to examine the fit and pronounced it satisfactory.

'All in order, Joe; we'll hire this little lot. Stick it on my bill, will you? I'll pick up my own gear from the locker on the way out, OK?'

Joe handed over a key. 'Help yourself, Charlie. Good diving.' He grinned appreciatively at Anthea.

Outside the shop Charles paused and looked around. Apart from the learners in the enclosed tank there were perhaps half a dozen people sitting at white tables in the annexe, and three or four couples sunbathing on the sand. A few snorkel tubes rose from the water like little periscopes as swimmers finned in leisurely fashion a short distance out from the edge of the tide. Further out a sailboard toppled slowly over, depositing its passenger into the water.

'Place is like Piccadilly Circus,' Charles said with disgust. 'Come on, we'll look for somewhere less cluttered.'

He loaded the gear into an open black Suzuki, and as Anthea climbed in beside him she said, 'Joe's quite a character, isn't he?'

'One of the best. As tough as they come. He came
here from Australia—used to have a diving school near
the Great Barrier Reef. He taught me all I know about
diving out there.'

He didn't volunteer any more information and
Anthea stole a glance at his stern profile as he waited
for a bus to pass before pulling out into the road. She
tried to think of something to say, but could only come
up with, Oh, did you live in Australia? which was
about as trite as you could get. So she said nothing.

When they were out on the road he said, keeping
his eyes straight ahead, 'I'd better warn you—I don't
indulge in nostalgia.' He must be a mind-reader.

That was her answer, then. OK, Mr Prickly Charles,
I won't bore you with small talk. I'm not very good
at small talk myself; I'd rather have large talk. She
giggled at the idea, and he slanted her a suspicious
glance but didn't deign to enquire what the joke was,
and the rest of the short journey was undertaken in
silence.

Anthea had expected that the drive would be more
or less the same distance that Peter had driven on his
way to the dive-shop, but the car passed the entrance
to the condos and went on and on.

When Charles finally drew into a small clearing
beside the road and parked the car, she said, 'Where
are we? We seem to have come miles.'

He was unloading the gear from the back seat.
'About seven miles, to be exact—the length of the
Seven Mile Beach.'

'The beach is seven *miles* long?'

'That's right.' He turned his mouth down at the
corners as he quoted, '"Seven miles of dazzling white,

white sand,'' the tourist brochures are fond of reminding one. But for once they're not exaggerating.'

He gave her the two pairs of fins to carry and
hitched the rest of the gear, together with a rug, over
one shoulder. 'Come and see for yourself.' He led the
way through a clearing bordered by palm trees and a
profusion of wide-leafed shrubs.

When they came out on to the beach Anthea drew
in a breath of delight. Miles of shimmering white sand
stretching in both directions, backed by luxurious
hotels and condo apartments—none more than tree-
top high—almost hidden from sight behind clumps
of pines and feathery bushes. Uncluttered, un-
crowded—the few people in sight were mostly in the
sea.

She turned to Charles, who was spreading a rug in
the shade of the bushes and unloading the diving gear.
'Paradise island, indeed!' she breathed. 'You know
it—you've been here before?'

His face became expressionless. 'Oh, yes, I've been
here before,' he said curtly. 'Now, you strip off and
then we'll get geared up.'

She'd walked straight into that—he'd warned her
that he didn't go in for nostalgia and she supposed
that meant no questions about the past. But the snub
hurt all the same.

Her fingers trembled as she undid the buttons of
her sun-dress. Charles divested himself of shorts and
shirt, disclosing narrow black swimming trunks which
showed his masculine shape beneath so explicitly that
Anthea looked away quickly.

Charles had no such delicacy. 'Very nice!' he said
with a grin, his eyes moving over her curves, barely
concealed by the citrus-yellow bikini.

She was surprised by the flirtatious tone of the remark. Up to now he hadn't shown any sign of wishing to flirt with her. He'd either been furious—or sarcastic, or arrogant, or, on that one occasion, curiously dejected. A lighter approach would make a nice change.

'Thank you,' she said and smiled at him.

The grin left his face as if it had been wiped off. He picked up her mask. 'See if you can get yourself into this,' he said shortly.

Anthea's spirits sank. Suddenly it seemed as if the sun had gone in. Clumsily she struggled to get the face-mask adjusted.

'Here—let me do it.' He eased the straps over her head and this time she noticed that his hands did not linger on her cheeks.

'OK, let's get going, then,' he said finally, picking up the two pairs of fins and starting off towards the sea, not waiting for her. Anthea stumbled after him, her feet sinking into the fine, warm sand. It was stupid to allow the man to have such a maddening effect on her, sending her spirits up and down like a crazy thermometer. She was beginning to wish she'd insisted on having her first lesson from one of Joe's instructors.

At the edge of the tide they stopped to fix the fins on their feet. 'Right,' barked Charles—rather like a drill-instructor, Anthea thought. 'Now the snorkel—fit the flange between your lips and gums and bite lightly on the two lugs. Breathe easily and naturally. We're just going to drift across the surface to get you accustomed to the finning movement and the feeling of keeping your face underwater. OK?'

Anthea nodded. She hadn't expected to feel so nervous; her insides were quaking. Then Charles took her hand firmly in his and they paddled together through the shallows, and suddenly all her nervousness left her. She was safe with him; he wouldn't let anything go wrong for her.

The water received her like a warm caress. She found herself following Charles's instructions automatically, letting her face dip into the sparkling, clear water, holding on to his hand as she imitated the slow, lazy finning movement of his strong legs.

At first she was hardly conscious of anything but the gentle gliding movement through the silky water. Then she realised that she had been keeping her eyes closed. When she opened them, the scene that appeared below was a magic fairyland.

Of course she'd seen films of the underwater world, but seeing it at first hand, through the amazing clarity of the sun-flecked water, was an entirely different matter. The forest of coral seemed so close, the shapes and colours so washed and fresh—sprouting tubes and crusted boulders and delicate spreading horns like those of some sea elk or reindeer. And the colours! Floating veils of weed in pinks and blues and greens around and between which tiny rainbow-coloured fish, striped and spotted, darted and wheeled as if intent on some secret and important business of their own.

Her hand was still held in Charles's hand and as they moved lazily through the water, finning in unison together, Anthea felt dreamily that they were sharing a wonderful experience and she wanted it to go on and on. But all too soon she felt a pressure on her arm, indicating that she should lift her head out of the water, as he did himself.

He removed his mouthpiece, and she followed suit. 'How's it going?' he asked, and she felt as if she herself were glowing all over with delight as she smiled at him.

'Marvellous! Unbelievable! Can we go on?' She wriggled her fins underwater as if she were one of the eager, purposeful small fish down there.

'Managing the breathing OK?' he asked, and she nodded impatiently. 'Right—we'll have another session,' he said. 'Take it easy.'

The second time was even better than the first. Anthea was confident now, well into the rhythm of the thing. She was fascinated by the way the fish disappeared into the little caves and inlets in the coral. Charles was not holding her hand now and she swam slowly beside him at her own pace.

Suddenly she spotted a large coral growth shaped like a shell, dimpled and pale blue, lying on the seabed. Its curved lower edge was raised slightly, forming the mouth of a dark cave, from which the face of a large fish peered out impassively as if viewing its own watery world. Anthea was captivated. She *had* to get a closer sight of this entrancing creature, which seemed to her fancy to be inviting her to examine his home. Impulsively she twisted her body and pushed downwards, finning as hard as she could.

She wasn't clear what happened next. She was conscious that the fish in the coral cave was much further down than she had thought. She pushed harder, automatically gulping in her breath. The next moment she was wildly churning up the water in an effort to get back to the surface. Her chest felt as if it were bursting.

What happened next had the quality of a nightmare. She was being dragged up to the surface and on to the sand; then the face-mask was off and the water was everywhere—blinding her, deafening her, pressing on her chest. She fought wildly for breath, retching and gulping as her head was pressed down and somebody—something—was thumping her back. She could hear horrible noises and knew it was her—she was dying. The thumping on her back got harder; a voice was shouting something but she couldn't make out the words.

Then, miraculously, she could breathe. She drew in a deep scratchy breath that hurt her chest and made a horrible noise in her throat. Another—and another—she *wasn't* going to die. She began to cry weakly.

Charles was kneeling beside her, his arm holding her. 'Better?' His voice sounded grim, angry.

She nodded, gasping in the warm, life-saving air, the tears pouring down her cheeks. Then she was scooped into his arms and he was carrying her back up the beach. It was wonderful to be held safe and close to the strong, warm body after the bleak moment of fear. She pressed closer, burying her cheek in the springy damp hair on his chest, listening to the loud beating of his heart. She wanted him to hold her like this for a long, long time.

He deposited her on the rug and wrapped a towel round her. Then he stood and looked down at her, frowning. She peered up at him miserably through her wet straggle of hair. 'What did I do wrong?'

'Just about everything,' he said unhelpfully. 'But let that pass. Now you stay here while I go along to the nearest hotel and rustle up a hot drink of some kind. Don't move,' he added fiercely.

As if she would! She watched him stride away across the sand and her eyes were wet still—but with tears of humiliation. It had been such a marvellous experience and she had made a fool of herself, and now Charles would certainly not bother with her again.

She bit her lip to stop it quivering, shocked to realise just how much that mattered to her.

CHAPTER FIVE

BY THE time Charles returned Anthea had pulled herself together. She had thrown the towel aside and stretched out on the rug. Her bikini was already dry in the hot afternoon sun, and her hair was drying rapidly too, spread out in a honey-brown tangle. Everything must be back to normal as soon as possible. No more panic. No more tears. No more clinging on to Charles. If he intended to drive her back to the condo and wash his hands of her—so be it, she thought, stiffening her pride.

He held out a plastic mug to her. 'It's not exactly five-star service but the kitchen staff were off duty for their afternoon break, and I had to persuade the receptionist to produce this. Drink up—it's the best possible antidote to shock.'

The sweet tea tasted good, washing away the taste of salt water that clung around her mouth. And there was a dash of something stronger in it, brandy probably. 'Thank you,' she said.

He lowered himself to the rug beside her and sat leaning back against the trunk of one of the tall palm trees that fringed the beach, his long legs thrust out before him. 'How are you feeling?' he said.

She glanced cautiously at him, trying to gauge his mood, but his face was expressionless.

'I'm fine,' she said. 'Thanks to you. Merely feeling ashamed of myself. I'm sorry to have behaved so idiotically.'

His long mouth pulled at the corners. 'We seem destined to apologise to each other.'

'What? Oh, you mean——'

'I mean we both appear to act on impulse now and again, and then regret it.'

'Two impulsive people!' she giggled. There must have been more brandy in the tea than she had realised. 'Sounds like the title of a song.'

'I can't admit to any excuse for my deplorable behaviour on the tennis court,' he said. 'What's *your* story?'

Anthea was beginning to get her confidence back. 'There was this fish...' she began, and she told him about the large fish peering at her from the opening to his coral cave. 'I didn't think,' she admitted. 'I just wanted to get down closer—to have a good look at him, and—and then I found I'd run out of breath and...'

He nodded. 'OK, I get the picture. I take a certain amount of responsibility. I should have explained to you the technique of breath-holding dives before we started. But I didn't expect you to start a love-affair with a fish.' He was smiling openly now, and Anthea grinned back at him, feeling a little light-headed because he wasn't angry, or dismissive, or patronising.

She finished the last drops of tea and put the mug down. 'Can we go in again now?'

He frowned, shaking his head. 'Oh, I don't think so. You've had a shock—you're not up to it.'

'Oh, I am, I am,' she wailed. 'I have to, don't you see? Don't you think it's better to—to start again straight away when you've had a set-back? Such as falling off your bike—you get on and try again straight away. If you don't you're left with the memory of failure.'

He was looking at her curiously, dark eyes hooded. 'Quite the psychologist, Miss Lloyd!'

'Heavens, no. It's just common sense.' She knelt up and reached for her face-mask. *'Please.'* She made a small gesture of pleading.

She wasn't prepared for what happened next. He stretched out and took her hand in a firm grip and pulled her down on the rug beside him.

'OK, you win,' he said. 'We *will* go in again, but not just yet. There are one or two things I want to say to you first.' His eyes narrowed in the lazy smile that pulled at her heart-strings. 'Are you sitting comfortably? No, you're not.' His arm went round her waist in a friendly way, pulling her against him.

For a moment she stiffened, then the touch of his hand on her midriff, the strength of his arm enclosing her, sent such a sensation of heady delight tingling through her that she relaxed weakly against him with a small sigh.

'That's more friendly,' he smiled.

He seemed quite content to sit there, holding her, and Anthea was content too—more than content: she was blissful. At last, this was the Charles she remembered, the hero of her youthful fantasies.

After a time he leaned his chin on the top of her head and said thoughtfully, 'You know, something you said just now hit me with a clang.'

Anthea murmured dreamily, 'Something I said?' and nestled a little closer. This was just the beginning, she thought. Very soon he's going to kiss me and then . . .

'Mmm—about getting on your bike again when you fall off. I had a bad tumble myself a short time ago, and instead of getting back on I sat by the roadside bristling at everyone who came near me, rubbing my wounds and feeling bloody sorry for myself. And, incidentally, sending my poor sister Nancy round the bend.'

Yes, the real Charles *was* still there, the man she'd idealised so long ago. She felt a leap of pleasure. It was as though she were meeting an old friend and finding he hadn't changed at all.

He went on thoughtfully, 'My sister is rather a special person and she has what she thinks of as my happiness and best interests at heart. For reasons which we won't go into, she thinks it would be good for me to get involved with a nice girl, to which end she's been applying herself for the past few weeks— first in London and now here. And nearly sending *me* round the bend,' he added drily, 'as you might have noticed.'

'Surely you——' Anthea began, but he held up a hand.

'Yes, I know, I could tell her what to do with her little plans, but I'd have to be fairly brutal to have any effect on Nancy. Once she's made up her mind to something it's not easy to shift her. And being brutal to Nancy doesn't appeal to me at all. For one thing I'm very, very fond of her. For another, she's trying valiantly just now to recover from the worst disappointment of her life. Losing a first, longed-for baby when you're over forty must be . . . well . . .' He spread out his hands, at a loss for a word.

'How wretched for her; I'm sorry,' Anthea said.

There was another pause. Where was all this leading? she wondered. If it was leading anywhere, that was.

'You see my difficulty?' he said. 'Nancy won't give up. I'm no psychologist but I imagine she may be concentrating all her disappointed maternal feelings on me. She'll be producing nubile young girls for me, like that red-headed siren Barbara she sent after me this morning when all I wanted to do was to get off on my own.' He groaned. 'God, how she chattered.'

Anthea said slowly, 'Was it Nancy who arranged for you to stop me from going diving with Peter?'

He quirked a dark eyebrow. 'Quick on the uptake, aren't you? I have to admit it was. It seems she was standing at her window and overheard your conversation with that young idiot, Peter. She—er—suggested I should come after the two of you and keep an eye on what was going on.'

'Really?' Anthea said distantly. 'I'm very sorry to have inconvenienced you and taken up your time.' She drew away from him and started to towel her hair vigorously.

'Don't be silly,' he said smoothly. 'On this occasion she didn't have to push me. I judged that caution was necessary. Nancy had gathered that the boy was a novice diver, and you can't be too careful. It's possible for accidents to happen, even when swimming or snorkelling—as you found out for yourself just now when you had your love-affair with the fish. Which brings me to what I was going to say. If you want to start an affair with anything—or anybody—while you're here, why not with me?'

For the second time in half an hour all the breath was knocked out of Anthea's body. She turned her head and goggled at him, but his eyes were closed.

'Joke?' she said.

'Not really.' He opened his eyes a fraction and they glittered in the sunshine like lines of jet under the heavy lids. 'How long are you here for?' He shot the question at her.

Taken off guard, she said, 'I plan to stay a fortnight or so.'

'A fortnight,' Charles mused. 'The same for me. That fits in splendidly.'

'Look,' Anthea said, dropping the towel and fumbling in her bag for a comb. 'I haven't the remotest idea what you're talking about. Or maybe I have.' She slid him a glance. It seemed out of character and totally contrary to everything that had happened, but if he really was making her a proposition she wanted nothing to do with it. It was too soon, too casual— oh, definitely no. 'If it's what I think it may be, the answer's no.'

He laughed aloud and it was the first time she'd heard him laugh—since that time five years ago. It was a good sound, deep and full-throated. 'You know, Anthea, I'm beginning to like you; I think we could be friends. And I doubt if I've ever said that to a girl before. No, as a matter of fact it *isn't* what you're thinking—and I know what that is. I'm not suggesting a sexual romp; just now I'm strictly celibate.' The hint of bitterness was back in his voice, but only for a moment.

He went on a little more quickly, 'I was merely suggesting a holiday friendship—destined like all holiday friendships to be a thing of the present. No past, no future, a fortnight of pleasure picked out of time. I thought we might find things to do together. We could explore the island, play tennis, go dancing. And I could teach you to dive—I'd like that. I promise to make you an expert in scuba by the end of a fortnight. What do you say?'

'I—don't know,' she said slowly.

What *did* she say? Could she spend two weeks in Charles's company without ending up completely besotted with him? And what would that bring her? Nothing but black misery. He'd been honest with her. He liked her—as a friend—but it was patently clear that some woman had dealt him an almost mortal blow quite recently. She—Anthea—would be a convenience. To let his sister think he had fallen for her would save him the hassle of having all these 'nubile young girls', as he called them, produced for him.

His eyes were fixed on her, and it seemed that he was following at least part of her train of thought.

'I admit I'm being entirely selfish,' he said. 'I should very much enjoy your company. But of course if you're looking for a——'

'A sexual romp? I'm not,' she said coolly.

'A man back in London?' he queried, tilting his head to one side.

'No, not any more.' She saw his lips firm and knew that he'd understood the message.

'Well, then, what about it?'

The questioning dark eyes seemed to be sending little trickles of electricity down her backbone. 'I . . .' she murmured uncertainly. Then slowly her mouth widened into a smile and her violet-blue eyes danced. 'I'd very much like to learn to dive,' she said.

He gave her an exuberant hug. 'Well said; I'll see that you do.' He got to his feet, picked up their snorkelling gear in one hand and pulled her up with the other. 'On your bike, girl.' His laughter rang out and was carried away by the breeze.

Running down the beach to the sea, hand in hand with him, Anthea suddenly felt a wild, surging happiness. There was just this moment, with the white sand warm to her feet, and the turquoise sea beckoning ahead, and this man beside her, her hand in his. As for the future, it could take care of itself.

'Happy now?' Charles asked quizzically, as they piled the diving gear into the back of his hired car an hour later.

Anthea collapsed into the passenger-seat with a long sigh. 'Blissful!' She raised shining eyes to his as he climbed in beside her. 'I was all right the second time, wasn't I?'

He let his glance travel over her flushed cheeks and settle on her lips, parted over even teeth as creamy white as peeled almonds. Then, for a fleeting second, they moved lower to the tender swell of her breasts under the green cotton dress. 'More than all right,' he said, a shade huskily, and turned the key in the ignition.

She said, 'I think I've found my natural habitat, as a Pisces girl—in the sea, of course. I could have gone on forever.' She slid him a wary glance. 'Or do you think star signs are all rubbish?'

He backed the car round and turned on to the road. 'At least I know what *my* star sign is.'

'Oh, let me guess.' Anthea sat back in the corner of her seat and subjected him to intense concentration. How lovely to have an excuse to do just that!

The strongly boned face, the autocratic nose, the sensual mouth—with just now a tolerant lift at the corners—the thick hair, drying into deep corrugations where he'd run his fingers through it. But most of all the eyes. Those hooded dark-as-night eyes. Magnetic. Hypnotic, almost.

She felt a deep shiver pass through her. You shouldn't tangle with a man who had eyes like that. You shouldn't agree to spend a 'platonic' fortnight with him. She remembered that violent moment on the tennis court when he'd let passion get the better of him. The man was a volcano—and if he erupted——

'Well? Made up your mind?' He slanted her an amused glance.

Anthea swallowed hard. 'Scorpio?' It had to be Scorpio.

He laughed aloud. 'Well, blow me down, the woman's a witch. How did you know?'

'Just a guess.' She wasn't going to admit to gobbling up magazine articles on the subject. Not until she knew him better, anyway. One thing she was remembering, and it was burning into her. That was that Pisces and Scorpio were marvellous together. She wouldn't mention that either.

She said quickly, 'When do I get my next lesson?'

'At the very first moment possible,' he told her. 'I have to see first if Nancy and Billy have anything arranged, but I'm darned sure Nancy will be ready to scrap any plans if she thinks you and I are going to get together. She'll be hearing wedding bells ringing loud and clear.' He chuckled as he swerved the car round a stationary bus.

Anthea stared straight ahead. 'It doesn't bother you at all that you're deceiving her? That she'll be disappointed when the charade is over at the end of a fortnight?'

She could sense the change in him, like frost settling over the clear surface of a pond. 'I don't look ahead as far as that,' he said shortly. 'And I'd suggest that you don't either.'

Of course—*no future*. He'd drawn the boundaries himself and she had to accept them or opt out altogether. She supposed it was kinder, really, to know the score from the start. She'd seen too many of her friends, back from romantic holiday affairs, waiting with painfully dying hope for letters and phone calls that didn't arrive.

She'd accept the reminder with good grace. 'OK,' she said cheerfully. 'Message received.'

He threw her a brief smile. 'Thanks, pal,' he said.

At least that seemed to cement the understanding between them—and the friendship too. It would have to be enough.

When they got back to the condo Charles left the car in the car park. 'I'll take the gear along to Joe's later,' he said. 'Everything has to be washed in fresh water and he has the facilities laid on. I've got a locker rented there and I'll put your stuff in with mine, OK?'

'Thanks.' She smiled warmly up at him. There was a good feeling about their sharing a locker. It meant that they were, in a way, a couple. Planning things, doing things together. How extraordinary that only two days ago Charles had been a distant memory, and now here he was beside her, and all the time he was becoming more like the Charles of her pin-up. Perhaps she hadn't been wrong about him, after all.

As they strolled round to the front of the building they saw Pamela and Nancy stretched out in basket chairs on the veranda. Charles threw an arm casually round Anthea's shoulder.

'May as well give the right signals.' He leant his dark head down to hers, whispering the words. She had an urge to rub her cheek against the rough masculine cheek so close to hers. Help! she thought. This wouldn't do at all. Friendship was all he had offered. She had to learn to think of him as—what? Not her type, not remotely sexy as far as she was concerned? Impossible, she decided wryly. The man was dynamite, so all she had to do was to be careful not to light the fuse.

Nancy beamed on them as they approached. 'Hello! And what have you two been up to?' she asked rather coyly.

They came to a halt in front of the veranda, still casually linked together. 'Charles has been giving me a lesson in snorkelling,' Anthea said. 'It was lovely, seeing all the coral and the fish and everything.' She stretched her arms above her head luxuriously.

Charles looked from Nancy to Pamela. 'She took to it like a mermaid,' he grinned. 'In fact, I think she must have been a mermaid in a previous incarnation.'

Anthea examined her neat ankles. 'No tail!' she remarked, and they all laughed.

The 'affair' was getting off to a good start, she thought, a nice, light-hearted atmosphere developing.

Nancy said, 'Guy and Bill have just arrived home. They're inside, fixing drinks.' She waved a hand over her shoulder.

'Splendid! I'll join them,' Charles said. 'What's yours, Thea?'

Thea! Wasn't it overdoing it a bit to coin a diminutive so soon? But she had to follow his lead, she supposed. 'Oh, something long and cool—and non-alcoholic,' she told him with a winning smile.

'Your wish is my command,' he grinned. Then he paused. 'That rings a bell. I seem to recall a poem in the *Golden Treasury*—a memory from my schooldays. It was called, "To Anthea, Who May Command Him Anything".'

OK, Anthea thought, if we're going to be whimsical I may as well join in. 'I must remember that.' She glanced up into the dark eyes, her own eyes dancing. 'It may be useful. Go and fix me a drink, slave.'

Charles went off to join the other two men and she sank into a chair. Nancy was looking the picture of satisfaction. Pamela, who hadn't spoken yet, was regarding Anthea's face with a slightly stunned expression.

She said, 'What happened to Peter? In your note you said...'

Anthea wrinkled her nose. 'Poor old Peter! He actually offered to teach me to dive when he'd only had one lesson himself. I didn't know how dangerous that might be. Fortunately Charles just happened to be at the dive-shop. He realised what was going on and took things in hand.'

She smiled innocently in Nancy's direction. 'Charles can be very masterful when he chooses, can't he? He said you can't be too careful where diving is concerned, and Peter took the hint and sort of—faded away. Then Charles very kindly offered to show me how to snorkel. And he's promised to give me my

first lesson in scuba diving later on.' As an explanation that was pretty thin—positively skeletal, she
thought with amusement.

'Oh! Oh, well, that's splendid,' Pamela said rather
lamely, and Nancy exclaimed,

'Yes, isn't it? Charles is a real expert, Anthea. I'm
sure you'll get on very well with him.' She smiled
happily, sinking back in her chair as the men arrived
with drinks.

Guy and Billy handed round the drinks and sat
down together, continuing a conversation about cur-
rency regulations. Charles brought his drink and
settled himself on the wooden floor of the veranda,
at Anthea's feet, leaning against the rail.

He looked up at his sister. 'Did you have anything
special in mind for tomorrow, Nan?'

Nancy leaned forward, wrapping her capable brown
hands round her glass. 'This evening we're bidden to
dine at Government House. Tomorrow—as Bill seems
tied up at the bank already—Pamela and I had an
idea that it would be nice if the four of us went out
to see a bit of the island in the morning—perhaps
take a picnic. That is, if you'd like to drive us?' She
was watching Charles a little warily, perhaps remembering how he'd reacted to her previous plans for him.
And no wonder, Anthea thought.

But Charles was all sweetness and light. 'Good
idea,' he said heartily. 'We'd like that, wouldn't we,
Thea? Then we could have our diving lesson later on
in the day.'

'Splendid!' Nancy beamed her approval, and began
busily to make arrangements with Pamela about the
time to start and who should organise the picnic.

Anthea met Charles's eyes and raised her eyebrows a fraction. Wasn't Nancy the least bit surprised at his sudden U-turn from introvert to extrovert? But he met her look with a bland expression which seemed to imply that his sister was a simple soul—easy to fool.

Anthea stood up abruptly. 'I think I'll go in now.' She smiled with particular warmth at Nancy. 'Thank you so much for the drink, Nancy, and I'll look forward to seeing you tomorrow.'

Without another look at Charles she escaped along the veranda and into the apartment next door. She supposed Charles knew Nancy, and knew what he was doing, but his ploy suddenly seemed trivial and selfish and she didn't relish being part of it. Also, she had a sense of let-down. She'd begun to think that she'd found again the Charles of five years ago—the ideal Charles she'd built up into a paragon of all the virtues. Of course, the fact was that she didn't really know the first thing about the man.

Feeling confused and rather cross, she peeled off her dress and bikini and went into the shower-room.

Anthea had expected that Pamela would remark on the rather sudden change in temperature between herself and Charles, from chilly to temperate—even warm. But when she went down to the living-room later, fresh from her shower and prepared with replies to any questions her sister might shoot at her, she found Pamela stretched out on the sofa, looking pale and languid. Guy was pacing up and down uneasily, and it was obvious that all was not well.

Guy came straight to the point. 'We've got a problem, Anthea. Our doctor called to do a routine check this afternoon and he's a little worried.' He paused behind the sofa and put his hands on his wife's shoulders. 'Nothing serious, he thinks, but he wants Pamela to fly to the mainland for a minor adjustment to be made. Something that he would be happier to have done in a larger hospital.' Guy was the most unflappable of men, but Anthea could sense that he was troubled.

She could feel the blood leaving her cheeks. 'Pam, darling, how rotten for you,' she said, trying to keep the alarm out of her voice.

Pamela smiled reassuringly at her. 'Don't worry, love, I'll be fine, and Guy will be able to come with me. Now that Billy's here he can take over Guy's job while he's away. Isn't that splendid?'

'Yes—yes, of course,' Anthea said in a small voice, pushing away all the horrid pictures that were creeping into her mind. Pamela desperately ill. Pamela losing the baby. Oh, no, *please*, she thought. Pam had always been so radiant, so lucky, so happy. It mustn't all be spoilt now.

She swallowed. 'When will you go?'

'Tomorrow, I'm afraid. The doctor phoned just a few minutes ago. He wasn't sure at first and he wanted to consult a very senior man in a Miami hospital before he said definitely that I ought to go.' Pamela stretched out a hand and Anthea grasped it and sank down beside the sofa. 'Poor love, it'll mean leaving you on your own here for a few days. Will you mind terribly?'

'Oh, for goodness' sake . . .' Anthea expostulated, 'don't bother about me! I'll be fine.'

Pamela turned to her husband. 'Darling, hadn't you better look in next door to tell Bill the news before they leave for their dinner party?'

When Guy had gone Pamela squeezed Anthea's hand. 'Now, you mustn't worry, love. I'm going to be perfectly OK. And you mustn't be lonely while we're away. Nancy's the kindest soul; I'm sure she'll be only too happy to stand in for me. And——' the brilliant blue eyes smiled into the violet ones conspiratorially '—isn't it splendid that you and Charles are hitting it off so much better?'

Anthea could have groaned. Now it wasn't only Nancy who'd got the wrong idea. It was Pamela too who would be hearing wedding bells.

Damn Charles Ravenscroft and his stupid play-acting. For two pins she'd tell Pamela the truth. She'd...

But, looking into her sister's beautiful face, so genuinely pleased and happily expectant, she couldn't do it.

She lifted Pamela's hand and rubbed her cheek against it. 'Get quite better quickly, Pam, dear,' she said. 'That's the important thing. Now, let me set about getting the meal that Juliana left for us. You just stay where you are—you're not to do a thing.'

As she made for the kitchen she couldn't help thinking that both her life and Charles's seemed to be complicated—for the moment—by having such very nice elder sisters. She hoped that neither of them would be too unhappy when their hopes were dashed at the end of the fortnight.

For herself, she refused to contemplate the end of the fortnight. *No future*, he'd laid down as a rule of the game, and she mustn't forget that, even for a moment.

CHAPTER SIX

IN SPITE of her doubts of the previous day, Anthea was glad of Charles's company next morning on the trip to Owen Roberts Airport. He had offered a lift in his hire car and Guy had accepted gratefully. They agreed it would be better than relying on a taxi.

The Suzuki could only seat four in comfort so Nancy stayed behind to see them off, to kiss Pamela and wish her luck over and over again.

As he piled the luggage in the boot Charles murmured to Anthea, who was helping, 'Poor old Nan, she's remembering only too well how things went for her.'

'Oh, *don't*,' Anthea gasped. 'Not Pamela, too!'

'Of course not,' he told her firmly. 'This is quite different. Your sister will be fine—she's got youth and everything else going for her. This is only a minor matter—Guy explained it to me. Now don't worry, sweetheart.' He closed the lid of the boot with a slam.

Anthea was comforted. This was the Charles she remembered—kind, encouraging, understanding. And he had called her 'sweetheart'. It wasn't much, but it sounded almost lover-like, the way he said it.

At the airport he took charge while Guy, much more white-faced and dithery than Pamela herself, hovered rather ineffectually.

'Poor darling, he's got the jitters,' Pamela chuckled to Anthea as they kissed goodbye outside Customs.

92

'Heaven only knows how he'll be when I'm actually having the baby.'

She turned to Charles. 'It was very good of you to give us a lift, Charles. And you promise to look after my little sister while I'm away?'

'I promise,' Charles said solemnly and kissed the cheek she held out to him.

What was that—a Judas kiss? Anthea allowed the thought to surface before she thrust it away again to join in the general goodbyes and arrangements to phone with news and telephone numbers when Guy had found a hotel.

She was silent as she walked with Charles to the car. As he headed back to town he said briskly, 'Cheer up, Anthea. Look, the sun's shining. I tell you what we're going to do. We're going back to the condo to have lunch with Nancy. After that you can have a rest and get into your swim-suit. I'll go along to Joe's to collect the scuba gear and you'll have your first real dive—and flirt with the fish as much as you like. How's that for a programme?'

'Fine,' Anthea agreed, trying to sound enthusiastic. Charles was being kind, but her mind was occupied with Pamela and what was going to happen at the hospital. A 'minor adjustment' Guy had called it. She wished she knew exactly what that meant—but of course even if she had known it wouldn't have helped. And minor operations sometimes went wrong, and . . .

The day went on just as Charles had planned. Nancy was already treating Anthea as one of the family— which gave her a nasty feeling of guilt—and lunch was a cosy affair, with Charles and his sister teasing each other and doing their best, not very successfully, to bring Anthea into the conversation.

'Now you must go and have a good rest,' Nancy told Anthea in a motherly voice when lunch was over. 'Then Charles will take you diving. That'll do you all the good in the world—take your mind off things.' She gave Anthea a conspiratorial smile and a friendly little push towards the next-door apartment.

It was grillingly hot in the bedroom and Anthea switched on the overhead fan, drew the curtains, peeled off her clothes and sank on to the bed. What a muddle everything was, she thought; and then, but what if Charles was really interested in her, and not putting on an act for his sister's benefit? What would happen next? He would find some place where they could be alone and he would take her in his arms and... Further than that she dared not imagine.

She closed her eyes and burrowed deeper into the soft mattress, pulled a flimsy coverlet over her as far as her waist, gave a long, deep sigh and almost immediately was asleep.

It was the strangest dream. She was back in her London flat and she and Charles were sitting at the table opposite each other. Between them was a dish on which reposed a large fish with shining blue and green scales. It was quite raw. 'Eat it up,' Charles was saying masterfully, 'it will do you good,' and she was weeping and pleading,

'I can't—I can't, please don't make me.' Then Charles got furious and started to thump on the table with a spoon.

Anthea opened her eyes with a start and realised that the thumping sound was someone knocking at the door. 'All right, I'm coming,' she croaked, sitting up and looking around for a wrap.

The bedroom door opened and Charles's dark head appeared round it. 'I couldn't get any answer downstairs...' he began. Then, as his eyes rested on the picture that Anthea made, sitting up naked in bed, he came further inside, grinning wickedly. 'Very nice,' he murmured. 'Very nice indeed!'

'Go away this instant!' Anthea grabbed the coverlet and pulled it up to her chin. He hadn't seen much more than was revealed by the top half of a bikini, but there was something about a bedroom that made the situation ridiculous and embarrassing.

He was still grinning as he went out and half closed the door. 'I'll wait downstairs,' he called back. 'Don't be long.'

Completely awake now, Anthea dived out of bed and slammed the door. Five minutes later, with a pink cotton skirt and top covering her white swim-suit, her bright hair brushed hastily and her feet thrust into white espadrilles, she ran downstairs.

Charles was standing at the window opening on to the veranda. 'Sorry to barge in just now,' he said, not looking at all sorry. 'I'd been knocking at the front door and began to wonder if you were OK when I couldn't get any answer.'

'I was perfectly OK,' Anthea said stiffly. 'I merely dropped off to sleep and didn't hear you. There was no excuse for you to walk into my bedroom.'

His raised eyebrow told her what he thought of such prudishness. She couldn't very well admit the truth: that, although she hadn't expected him to leap on her when he saw her naked, it was somewhat deflating that he found her sex appeal a minus quantity. Or, rather, a joke, which was even worse.

Then all of a sudden she saw the funny side of it and began to giggle. 'As a matter of fact I was dreaming about you,' she said.

His eyes widened. 'Go on—tell me.'

'You were trying to make me eat a raw fish and when I wouldn't you began to bang on the table with a spoon. That must have been when you were banging on the door.'

Her dancing eyes invited him to see the joke. But he wasn't smiling. He was looking at her intently and rather oddly, a cloud of bewilderment passing over his face.

Then it cleared and he grinned slowly. 'You've got quite a thing about fish, haven't you?' he teased. 'Come on, let's go and search for some in their natural habitat. I've got all the necessary gear in the car.'

They went out on to the veranda. 'No need to lock up here—there aren't any thieves in the Caymans, unless you count the ones in the big banks. With apologies to our respective brothers-in-law, who wouldn't see the joke.'

As they got into the car Anthea said idly, 'You aren't in banking yourself, then? I took it for granted...'

The dark eyes raked her with cold deliberation. 'It's safer to take nothing for granted,' he said curtly, and she could almost hear the ice crackling in his voice.

When they were both seated he didn't start the car immediately. One hand on the key and the other gripping the wheel, he said, 'Suppose we keep our conversation limited to the present moment—as I think I suggested.'

She stared at his hand on the wheel. The knuckles were white with tension—or was it anger? Back to square one, she thought despondently. How could she ever get used to this Jekyll and Hyde individual? She drew herself up and said stiffly, 'Very well, but if I forget, and occasionally behave like a normal human being, you'll just have to remind me.'

He relaxed, sighing deeply. 'I'm sorry, Anthea. You deserve better. If you want to call it off...'

She went cold. She'd accepted his terms and she knew the risk, but there was always hope and she wasn't going to give up yet.

She managed a laugh. 'Call it off? Certainly not. What about my love-affair—with the fish?'

'Yes, there is that.' He joined in the laugh but neither her laugh nor his would have convinced a third party. 'Come on, then, let's write the next chapter in the Girl Meets Fish saga.' He started the car.

In the days that followed, Guy's phone messages were reassuring. Pamela had come through the 'minor adjustment' satisfactorily and she was well and cheerful—although ordered bed-rest in hospital for the time being. Relieved of anxiety, Anthea threw herself with all her new energy into the challenge of learning everything Charles could teach her about scuba diving.

At the end of the holiday she would go back to London, to the endless chores of finding new premises, buying new equipment, working on new designs. But all that was in another world and she refused to think about it.

Perhaps, in a way, she and Charles were a pair, both of them using this fortnight's holiday to dispel the traumas of the past. The difference was that he was making it plain that she didn't figure in his future, whereas she . . . she was daily feeling more and more disturbed by his physical presence.

But he made no move towards her. Even when they were with Nancy and Bill he never touched her. For Nancy's benefit they were supposed to be getting seriously interested in each other—that was the ploy. Then surely it would have been more convincing if Charles had delivered a casual hug or kiss now and then? But no, he kept his distance. Sadly she decided that he must be making quite sure that at the end of the fortnight there would be no messy emotional parting.

Each day they drove out to Charles's favourite quiet beach, and each day Anthea became more skilled in the techniques of scuba diving. Her underwater dives with Charles as partner were intoxicating. When she was confident enough they swam further out, beyond the reef that divided the turquoise lagoon from the darker, deeper sea beyond. Sitting on a coral reef under fifty feet of water, stroking sponges and playing hide-and-seek with exotic fish round the pink and green trumpets of coral, was definitely an other-world experience.

She was learning all the time—learning the names of the fish they met: yellowtail snappers, striped sergeant fish, delicate blue and silver butterfly fish, friendly angel fish. She was learning other things too—the underwater sign-language divers used to talk to each other, the techniques of descent and ascent, the drill in case of emergencies, the use of compass, depth gauge, and wrist-watch to record time spent underwater.

But of course they couldn't spend all the days diving and learning about diving. Some mornings they played tennis, at other times they went on what Charles called the 'tourist trail'.

Anthea tried to persuade Nancy to join them on their expeditions, but she always found some excuse. She had shopping to do, she was meeting Bill for lunch in town, she had to wait for the maid to arrive.

So Charles and Anthea went together. They wandered round George Town, which seemed to Anthea mainly composed of gleaming banks and offices, as well as smart and expensive shops. They duly visited the district called Hell, where a wooden walkway crossed the jagged black rocks that gave the place its name—and from where one could send cards postmarked 'Hell' to one's friends and relations, with facetious messages. One day they drove out to the unique turtle farm at West Bay. Their stay at the turtle farm was very brief because Anthea couldn't bear to look at all the fascinating creatures swimming happily in their watery homes, from tiny babies to fully grown adults, without visualising their inevitable end—their beautiful shells appearing as trinkets in gift-shop windows, and what was beneath their shells as tasty items on restaurant menus.

Charles teased her for being squeamish but she argued stoutly for her point of view. There were lots of things they argued about and many tastes they shared. He was a delightful companion, fun to be with, outgoing and yet—curiously remote.

Guy telephoned every morning before Anthea went out, and once Anthea was able to talk to Pamela herself. She was fine, she said, and longing to get home. How was everybody, and was Anthea managing to have a good holiday? And was Juliana turning up as arranged?

'Oh, fine, fine,' Anthea bubbled in reply to all the questions. She'd given Juliana a holiday, as her mother was ill. Nancy was being so kind and had insisted on Anthea's having dinner with them each evening. Bill had taken them all out one night to dinner at the Royal Palms—terribly posh! There was a suggestion that they might book for a trip in the submarine to see the underwater scene by night—it sounded fabulous!

'And how about Charles?' Pamela questioned, when Anthea had run through all her news without mentioning him. 'Are you two seeing much of each other? And do you like him any better? Don't hold out on me, love,' she pleaded, half laughing but unashamedly agog for news.

'Charles is teaching me to dive,' Anthea told her. 'He's an excellent teacher and we're getting along quite well. And that, sweet sister, is all there is to tell. So don't think any more about a rich husband for me, there's a dear. There's nothing doing in that direction.'

'Oh!' Pamela's disappointment travelled clearly along the telephone wire. 'Oh, well, you never know.'

I know, Anthea thought, as she said goodbye and put down the receiver. Only too well.

Each evening at dinner Charles regaled his sister and brother-in-law with Anthea's progress in scuba diving. He was delighted with his pupil, and Nancy was quite obviously delighted with the state of affairs.

'Charles is so much happier,' she confided to Anthea. 'You two nice people really do hit it off marvellously, don't you?'

Do we? Anthea wondered as she murmured some sort of response. What sort of 'hitting it off' was it when a man and a girl spent hours together every day without any personal conversations, without once touching each other? The worst of it was that she found herself longing more and more for him to touch her, letting her gaze dwell on his mouth, his hands, and being utterly unable to stop herself imagining how it would be to be in bed with him. What was this? It couldn't be love, not in just a few days—you couldn't count that teenage crush five years ago. So it must be plain lust, which thought did nothing for her self-esteem. To yearn for a man who never laid a finger on her was humiliating.

But Charles had made the rules. Friendship and companionship for two weeks, then—finish! And definitely no sex.

As the blue and gold days followed each other she felt she was living on borrowed time. The days were racing past much too quickly.

Eleven days of the fortnight gone—three days left.

Anthea groaned as she counted the shrinking hours. She had three days to—to what? To make him fall in love with her? Not a hope, she told herself dismally. And it was a waste of time kidding herself that it was merely lust she felt for the man. She was in love with him, deeply, painfully in love. The time dragged heavily when they were apart. Her insides squeezed up tight when she saw him coming towards her. She only came alive when they were together. She didn't know how she was going to continue to live when the fortnight was over.

* * *

'What about this, then?' Charles inspected the tiny rock-bound cove with approval. 'So there really *is* a deserted beach in Grand Cayman. Not just quiet, as the tourist adverts say, but definitely deserted.'

'Just in time—I couldn't walk another yard.' Anthea flopped down on the sand in the shade of a coconut palm, hugging her knees, which were encased in pink linen jeans to protect her legs from the intense heat of the afternoon sun and the possible attack by sand-flies. For the same reason she wore a loose long-sleeved top of pink lawn. She was browning nicely but she still had to be careful, and it was easier to cover herself up than to have to plaster sun-block cream all over her body as usual.

This morning had been occupied by the daily diving lesson and this afternoon Charles had suggested a change. They had driven up towards the north of the island and from then on Anthea had been quite lost. They had lunched, in a little restaurant with a thatched roof, off a superb seafood dish followed by ice-cream laced with tropical fruit. They had parked the car when the road ran out and then made their way slowly—very slowly—through a mini-jungle bordering a swamp forest. The trees, plants, crabs and exotic parrots were all part of the magic, and it hadn't seemed to matter that in places the swamp slopped over on to the path and they had had to proceed barefoot.

And then, suddenly, they had come upon this little cove, where the breeze off the ocean was cool and the waves creamy, and the leaves of the coconut palms rustled above them.

'I don't know about you,' Charles said lazily, 'but I'm going to have a kip.' He flung himself down and

lay back on the soft sand, hands behind his head.
'Poke me if I snore.'

'You bet I will,' Anthea promised. That was the
way it was with them—friendly, jokey. She might have
been his much younger sister.

He was asleep almost immediately. Anthea lay back
beside him, took off her sunglasses and closed her
eyes, but sleep was a long way away. She was tinglingly
aware of the long body of the man stretched out beside
her. She moved a little further away but it was no
better. It seemed that there was a magnetic current
between them, drawing her towards him. She lifted
herself on an elbow and let her eyes roam over him,
over the strong-boned face, the dark hair, rumpled
and clinging damply to his forehead, the thick lashes
curving on to his cheek, the long, straight upper lip
resting lightly on the full lower lip, the broad, square
chin.

Her insides moved painfully. She loved him so very
much. She wanted him with a desperation that
shocked her. And she knew nothing about him.
Nothing except a bit of gossip via Pamela about a
broken love-affair. It must have been a deeply
passionate, tragic affair to have made him choose a
monk-like existence as he seemed to have done.

Her gaze travelled down his body, clad in a cotton
vest and navy shorts that fitted tightly across his hips.
Masculine, virile, powerful—those were the words that
came into her mind. Yet they had spent hours together
in this romantic sun-kissed island, and, except for that
dance together when they'd dined with their respective families, and the time he'd hauled her out of
the water on her first dive, he'd never even touched
her—only when they were under the water together.

Any other man she'd met would at least have made
a pass by now. Was he really heartbroken? Or was he
married? But no; if he was married surely Nancy
would know and wouldn't keep it a secret.

He had the dark skin that tanned quickly and easily,
and in the shade of the trees his arms and legs were
the colour of teak. Anthea couldn't tear her eyes away
and her heart began to beat heavily.

Her arm moved without her willing it; she put her
hand on his thigh and she drew in a long shaky breath
as a wave of heat passed through her that had nothing
to do with the sun.

The heavy lids lifted and he looked straight up into
her bemused blue-violet eyes. 'Why don't you?' he
said lazily.

She knew what he meant. It was an invitation but
it was up to her—he wasn't going to make the first
move. Slowly, never taking her eyes from his, she
lowered her head and put her mouth on his.

For a long, frightening moment she thought he
wasn't going to respond. Then his arms came up and
drew her down beside him until their bodies were
touching. His lips stroked hers gently backwards and
forwards and she felt a rising tide of longing and
opened her mouth...asking...needing. When she
felt his tongue seeking hers a shudder of delight passed
through her. She had never felt like this before—
wanton, eager, aflame with desire. Her arms went
round his neck, burying themselves in the thick hair,
pulling him closer until he was lying half on top of
her.

His tongue probed delicately, exploring the warm
crevices of her mouth, savouring, tasting. His hands
stroked her shoulders, her back, moving down over

her hips, lightly, almost tentatively. There was no passion to match her own; he might have been an expert savouring a new wine, running it experimentally round his mouth.

A sob broke in her throat. 'Charles—Charles, darling,' she muttered. 'Please...' Her arms went round his waist pulling him down on to her.

Then everything changed. He was kissing her with crazy passion, breathing harshly, his hands fumbling for the zip of her jeans, his body, hard and aroused, moving on hers with a rhythm that shocked and thrilled her, setting up an ache in her loins that cried out for satisfaction. She heard a whimpering sound and hardly realised she was making it.

She couldn't believe it when he thrust himself away, rolling off her, gasping and fighting for control. Then, without a word, he got to his feet and staggered to the edge of the tide. She stared numbly, seeing him pull off shorts and shirt and plunge, naked, into the water. His arms gleamed brown above the turquoise of the lagoon as he struck out in a fast crawl for the line where waves were breaking over the reef.

Anthea was shaking all over. Her head felt like cotton wool, her limbs like jelly. All she was conscious of was humiliation like a great lump of lead inside her, so agonising that she could hardly bear it.

Time crawled by. If she could have got up and walked away from the beach she would have done so. But she doubted if her legs would bear her, and anyway she couldn't remember where the path was. Somewhere they had pushed their way through a thicket of bushes to reach this private cove but, looking round, she could see no opening.

Charles was a long way out from the beach now, swimming powerfully towards the open sea. Watching him, Anthea felt a tug of fear. He wasn't going to...he couldn't...

She wasn't thinking straight at all. All she remembered was the violence in him, the storm that had passed over him, turning him into a different man. A desperate man. Why? *Why?* she thought, but the only answer was that it was her fault; she had brought it on herself.

She fixed her eyes on the dark head that was now only a speck on the darker blue water beyond the reef, watched with a clench of fear in her stomach until she saw it coming nearer and knew he was swimming back to the cove.

When he stepped out of the water at the edge of the tide and stood very still, his body bronzed and perfect, he seemed to her like primitive man, glorying in his nakedness. Like Adam in his lonely garden—before Eve appeared to tempt him. She began to laugh helplessly, burying her face in her hands. And then, because she had first been stirred to the depths and afterwards scared out of her wits, the laughter turned to tears. She choked and gulped helplessly, the tears running through her fingers, her shoulders shaking.

'Anthea—stop it. Stop it this minute.' The words, barked out in the voice of a sergeant major, arrested her hysteria instantaneously. Without taking her hands from her face, she could see a pair of strong bronzed legs, dark hairs clinging wetly to them. She blinked the tears from her eyes and let her gaze travel further up, and saw that he'd pulled on his navy shorts. His vest lay in a crumpled heap where he'd flung it down on the sand.

He wrenched her hands from her face. 'What's the matter? Why the waterworks?' he asked irritably.

He had the nerve to ask her that just as if nothing had happened! She turned her head away. He was making her feel small and insignificant, looming above her. She wanted to spring to her feet and tell him what she thought of him, but she had no spring left in her and she was sure the words wouldn't come.

'Anthea—look at me!' He was down on his haunches beside her now. His hand grasped her chin and turned her face roughly towards him. She put every ounce of effort she was capable of into stopping her mouth from shaking and meeting the accusing dark eyes squarely.

They stared at each other in silence. 'Look,' he said at last. 'It's not the end of the world because I kissed you.'

'Was that all it was?' she asked stonily.

He released her chin and slumped round until he was sitting beside her, staring bleakly out to sea. 'All right,' he said at last. 'I lost my head. I'm only human and my control isn't as good as I thought it was. If I alarmed you, I'm sorry,' he added stiffly, 'but I don't take all the responsibility, you know.'

Anthea lifted her chin a fraction. 'It seems that I'm only human too.'

He ignored that. 'I should never have started this game—it was a stupid thing to do.' He reached for a small stone and hurled it violently into the water. 'I told you—I warned you that I couldn't offer you a romantic holiday affair, with a spice of sex thrown in.' He turned towards her and his face was grim. 'In case you're getting any wrong ideas I may add that I'm *not* impotent, I'm *not* a health risk.' He bit out the words savagely. 'And I'm *not* going to get myself involved in any emotional entanglement.' He paused and added, 'That's the way things are.'

'OK, OK,' Anthea put in coldly. 'So I broke your precious rules. It won't happen again, I promise. Perhaps the less we see of each other for the next three days the better. Anyway, Pamela is coming home tomorrow. I told Nancy—did she tell you?'

'Yes, she did. I got the impression that Pamela, too, would be delighted to find that you and I are— to use Nancy's words—getting on so well together.' His mouth twisted hatefully. 'It seems that your sister Pamela has hopes for us too.'

Anthea dug up a handful of sand and let it trickle through her fingers. She sensed the violence seething just under the surface of Charles's words, and it frightened her. Somehow this conversation must be diverted into less dangerous channels.

She forced a brittle laugh. 'Pamela thinks I should find myself a rich husband—like hers.'

'I see. And does your sister think I would fit the bill?'

She didn't like the look in his eye. Did he know he was twisting a knife inside her? No, of course he didn't. 'Love' was a word that had never been mentioned between them.

But there was still pride. She shrugged. 'Well, I suppose she'd consider you about right. I'm sure you're absolutely stinking rich, aren't you? Oops— sorry! I'm not allowed to ask you that, am I?'

His expression hardened. 'No,' he said, 'you're not.' He got to his feet. 'Now, suppose we make our way back, and do our best to put this not very admirable episode behind us as if it hadn't happened?'

She scrambled up. 'Suits me,' she said in a carefully offhand tone.

As she followed him through the thick bank of prickly bush on to the path she saw that her arms were scratched and bleeding, but she didn't feel any pain. All the pain in the world seemed to be concentrated in her heart.

CHAPTER SEVEN

'SO PAMELA is coming home tomorrow.' Nancy smiled at Anthea over the rim of her coffee-cup. 'Won't it be lovely for you to have her back?'

'Lovely,' Anthea agreed enthusiastically. It *would* be lovely to see Pam again. It was the only good thing in an otherwise bleak prospect.

She had contemplated making some excuse to get out of joining Nancy, Bill and Charles for dinner at their usual restaurant, close to the condo. But Nancy had been worrying about the scratches on Anthea's arms and had insisted on giving first aid with antiseptics and bandages. If she'd pleaded a headache or some other minor symptom Nancy would have jumped to all sorts of dire conclusions about poisonous tropical plants, would have insisted on calling a doctor, would have treated her as an invalid and would have generally behaved like the kind, motherly soul she was.

So Anthea had decided that it was simpler to join them for dinner. Afterwards she would go straight back to Pamela's apartment, explaining that she wanted to have everything ready for Pamela's return. That would ensure that at no point in the evening would she risk being alone with Charles.

He had suggested putting this afternoon's episode behind them as if it hadn't happened, but it seemed that neither of them was capable of doing that. As they sat next to each other at the small restaurant table

Anthea felt the tension between them like an electric filament, ready to burn white-hot at the touch of a switch. He had been silent over the meal in spite of his sister's efforts to draw him out about the afternoon's expedition, and it had fallen to Anthea to describe the walk through the marshy jungle and the way they had finally found the little deserted cove.

She flicked a glance at Charles's dark unsmiling face as she talked. The very least he could have done was to help her out, she thought crossly. He seemed to have reverted to the mood he'd been in when they'd all had dinner together that first night. The restaurant was full—mostly with bank staff and their families. Anthea let her gaze wander over the other tables, exchanging smiles with one or two people she had already met. Peter Jordan was there with a party— his parents presumably and several others, including the red-haired siren Barbara, who was chatting away vivaciously, telling some story, embellished by much waving of her hands and arms. Peter didn't seem to be listening. His long body was slumped over the table, fingers playing listlessly with his wine glass.

As he caught Anthea's glance he brightened and lifted a hand. Since the episode at the dive-shop she had encountered Peter several times. He had hopefully issued invitations—to play tennis, to go sailing, to drive round the island—and always Anthea had refused tactfully. Finally he seemed to have given up hope.

But this evening, annoyance with Charles put brilliance into her smile as she returned Peter's salute. She saw his immediate response. He straightened his long body, pushed back his flop of fair hair, stood up and loped across to their table.

'Good evening, Mrs Jamieson—Mr Jamieson.' He nodded vaguely towards Charles and flushed as his gaze moved to Anthea. 'I was wondering—Barbara and I are going on to the new night-club that's just opened along the beach...' He gestured across his shoulder. 'Would any of you care to join us? They've got a live band and there's dancing; it sounds as if it may be fun.'

Nancy beamed on the tall young man. 'I'm afraid Bill and I are too old-fogeyish for night-clubs, aren't we, darling?' She squeezed her husband's shoulder and he patted her hand, nodding urbanely, eyes twinkling behind their gold-rimmed glasses.

'But I'm sure Charles and Anthea would love to join you, wouldn't you, my children?' Nancy went on skittishly, but with a wary glance at Charles.

Anthea had a wicked urge to stir Charles out of his dark mood, or at least to challenge it. '*I* would,' she said brightly. 'How about you, Charles?'

To her amazement he agreed laconically, 'Why not?' He got to his feet. 'Come along, then, we'll join them.'

Oh, lord, what had she done? She'd have to dance with him, be held against him. And what effect would that have on her? If she was close to him she might have an overwhelming urge to press closer still. And then—if he thought she hadn't given up, that she was issuing another invitation to him? Oh, God, she couldn't bear it. To be slapped down once was enough.

She looked pleadingly towards Nancy, willing her to enquire about the scratches on her arms, to ask whether she was *sure* she felt like making a night of it. But Nancy was exchanging small talk with Peter

about his parents, her dark eyes—so like Charles's—
alive with animation below the straight-cut fringe.

'Go along, then, both of you, and have a lovely
time. Bill and I will be fast asleep when you come in,
Charles, but the door will be open.' Nancy cast a
faintly coy glance towards her brother. To Anthea's
fevered imagination she seemed to be saying that if
he and Anthea chose to spend the night together while
the apartment next door was conveniently empty of
its owners, nobody would be asking any questions.
Little did she know!

Anthea walked between Peter and Charles to the
table where Barbara was already getting to her feet,
her eyes resting greedily on Charles.

'Charles—you're coming with us? Brilliant!' She
linked an arm with his. 'How marvellous—we're look-
alikes.' She gurgled with laughter, indicating the min-
uscule caramel-coloured dress that seemed cleverly
almost to disappear into her smooth, delicately
browned skin, and then ran a finger slowly down the
front of Charles's thin khaki shirt, her eyes dancing
up to his, the tip of her tongue touching her lips.

He wouldn't stand for that sort of obviousness,
surely? Anthea thought in disgust. But while he
greeted the other members of the party briefly, he allowed the girl's arm to remain in his, and smiled down
at her with apparent pleasure as they walked towards
the exit door, leaving Anthea to follow with Peter.
The night-club, he told her, was attached to one of
the big hotels on Seven Mile Beach, only a couple of
hundred yards from the restaurant where they'd been
dining.

Outside, the sky was like black velvet, spattered with
glittering diamond-clusters of stars. Lights from the

hotels and apartment buildings gleamed through their protecting trees and shrubs on to the endless vista of white sand. Long, pencil-straight lines of waves turned over quietly, as if reluctant to disturb the peace.

'Not worth taking a car,' Peter said. 'Let's pull off our shoes and wade along with the crabs.' He sounded rather psyched up, Anthea thought, and wondered how much wine he'd drunk with dinner.

Barbara squealed, 'Oh, no, not crabs!' and clung on tightly to Charles.

'Silly girl, there aren't any crabs,' Charles told her, playfully tolerant. 'Come on, get those pretty little sandals off.' He had his arm round her waist and she raised her feet, one after the other, for him to remove her sandals, leaning against him, giggling that he was tickling her.

Anthea moved from the edge of the tide on to dry sand. She was not going to take part in such childish games. She glowered towards the two in front. 'I thought Barbara was with *you*,' she said to Peter, drawing away as she felt his arm encircle her waist.

'She was—until she found something better. So I'm afraid you'll have to put up with the discard, sweetie.' He chuckled as his arm came to rest more firmly round her waist.

Sweetie! That wasn't Peter's style. And when his face came close to hers she recoiled. He certainly *had* been going at the wine.

'Come on,' she said, striding out determinedly. 'Show me where this night-club is.' She couldn't help it if she let him see her lack of enthusiasm. That was how she felt. She'd been worrying about how she was going to respond to Charles in the intimate atmosphere of a night-club. She needn't have bothered, she

thought viciously, glancing over her shoulder to where
he was skipping in and out of the waves, with the red-
head clinging to his arm and shrieking playfully.

Inevitably she and Peter reached the night-club first.
He found a table by the window and ordered drinks
from a gorgeous dark-skinned girl in a scarlet tunic
with a white carnation in her hair. The whole room
was decorated in scarlet and white and glowed like a
gigantic jewel in the coloured lighting. On a dais near
the bar a five-piece band was playing top-ten music
and one or two couples were moving together on the
postage-stamp dance-floor.

Barbara came rushing in, attractively breathless,
green eyes dancing with fun, and flopped into a chair.
'Isn't this *brilliant*? Oh, look, Charles, they're going
to do a floor-show. Come and sit by me.' She patted
the chair next to her. 'Yes, I'd simply love a drink—
just anything you'd like to choose.'

She didn't even glance at Peter. She had, as he had
ruefully admitted, found something better.

Apparently Charles, too, had found something
better, Anthea thought sourly. It was obvious that he
was showing her that their little charade was over—
she had spoilt it. But he needn't have been quite so
obvious about it. In the disco lights that roved around
the room and over the colourful gyrating bodies of
the dancers in the floor-show she caught glimpses of
Barbara and Charles like fleeting images in a pop
video—Barbara rubbing her cheek like a kitten against
Charles's silk khaki shirt, his arm round her shoulders,
his dark head bent to hers.

Anthea gulped down her drink, trying to blot out
the misery, and was hardly aware that Peter's arm was
drawing her closer, that the bottle of wine he'd or-

dered was nearly empty and that his hand was straying down towards the hem of her skirt.

The floor-show ended, the band went off for their break, and disco music belted out. Barbara pulled Charles on to the floor and was soon jiving and twisting enticingly for his benefit, while he was content to move his body rhythmically to the beat without trying anything fancy. Anthea couldn't take her eyes off the two of them and a smouldering resentment burned inside her, somewhere between her throat and her stomach. Her head was starting to ache as the decibels from the loudspeakers boomed in her ears. Barbara was showing off, executing a complex dance movement, during which she managed to trip and fall, apparently by accident, into Charles's arms. Before he set her straight he dropped a kiss on her flaming red hair.

'Like to have a go?' Peter shouted over the noise. 'I'm not much good, but——'

'No, thanks,' Anthea shouted back hastily. 'I'd much rather stay here and watch.'

'Suits me.' His voice was slurred, and the hand at the hem of her skirt was groping its way upwards into more intimate territory.

'Please don't.' She grabbed his hand and removed it. It felt damp and limp. 'I—I'm awfully sorry, Peter, but I don't feel too good. Would you mind very much if I went back to the apartment?'

'Course not—come with you,' he said immediately.

'I'll be OK, really, if you'd like to stay,' she said. To get away on her own—away from the heat and the lights and the heavy beat of the music, and the sight of Charles with that girl—that was what she wanted. But Peter was basically a kind boy and she wouldn't hurt his feelings, so when he stood up rather un-steadily and held out his hand she went with him.

Outside, the air was cool and the sound of the shallow waves lapping against the sand was soothing. Anthea drew in a deep breath.

'Feeling better?' Peter's voice was steadier. Perhaps the fresh air had got to him too.

'Yes, thanks. I don't think night-clubs are quite my scene.'

'Not mine either,' he said rather glumly. 'I guess I'm an outdoor type.'

He linked his arm with hers. 'I hope I didn't . . . I wasn't . . .' he began awkwardly. 'I'd had too much wine.'

'Don't give it a thought,' Anthea assured him. She realised now that he was painfully shy and he'd been going through the motions of what he thought was expected of him. She felt an affection for him that was almost maternal. In a funny sort of way she understood what Nancy felt for Charles.

Charles! Charles was a very different matter. Charles wasn't shy—merely callous and self-absorbed and . . . and despicable!

'Tell me about your college,' she said to Peter. 'What games are you best at?'

Released from the necessity of putting on a macho act, Peter relaxed and chatted away about his hopes of getting into the second cricket eleven and taking up rowing next term.

At the front door of the condo he hesitated. 'Will you be OK on your own? Your sister's away, isn't she?'

'I'll be fine,' she assured him. 'The air's almost taken my headache away.'

He looked down at her from his great height. 'I'd hoped…' he began awkwardly. Then, 'It's that fellow Charles, isn't it? I've seen you about together and . . .'

She didn't pretend to misunderstand. Peter was a straightforward boy and he deserved a straight-forward reply. 'No, it isn't Charles; it isn't anybody really,' she said, and added, 'There's someone back at home, you see.' That white lie seemed excusable.

She pushed the door open, but when Peter seemed rooted to the spot she said, 'I'll be going back to London in a couple of days, but I expect I'll see you before I leave. Thank you for looking after me this evening—I'm sorry I had to cut it short. Goodnight, Peter.' She reached a long way up and planted a kiss on his cheek.

'Oh . . .' It was too dark to see his face but she was sure he was blushing. 'Goodnight, Anthea. You're a— a marvellous sport,' he stammered.

She went in and closed the door, locking it. People seemed careless about locking their doors here, but somehow the act of turning the key was symbolic, as if she were finally shutting out the fruitless longing for Charles.

The thought of bed appalled her. She went up to the bedroom, pulled off her clothes and got into a flowery wrap of wild silk that Pamela had lent her. Downstairs again, she made a pot of tea and carried it to the sitting-room. Here she drew the curtains and switched on a reading lamp and picked up one of Pamela's paperback thrillers. It had a cover picture of a posy of lilies of the valley, beside which was a lethal-looking knife spattered with blood. She put the book down with a shudder. Extraordinary how a mild, sweet, loving woman like Pamela should be addicted to horror stories. You never really understood people, did you?

A loud banging on the door made her jump and catch her breath. The thought of blood-stained knives was still occupying her mind ghoulishly. She froze. Nobody she knew would bang like that—certainly not Nancy or Bill.

The banging stopped and then—oh, heavens!— heavy footsteps sounded on the veranda and impatient knocking on the window.

She got to her feet, her knees like putty, and sidled across the room. Tweaking the outer edge of the soft velvet curtain, she put one eye to the gap. A detective in a TV serial would have been proud of her, she thought hysterically.

Outside, in the starlight, Charles's large body was immediately recognisable. Gibbering with relief, Anthea pulled back the curtains and unlatched the sliding glass door.

He strode into the room, glowering into every corner. 'Where is he?' he barked.

Anthea collapsed on to the sofa. 'Where's who? What are you talking about? And how dare you come barging in like this?' she added as an afterthought.

'Where's that dressed-up drink of water? I'll——'

'If you're referring to Peter, he very kindly brought me home, said goodnight, and left.' Suddenly all the humiliation of the afternoon and evening came back in a rush. She sat up very straight and glared at him as he stood by the open window like an animal at bay. 'And what business is it of yours?' she said in a steely voice. 'You were too happily occupied yourself to notice what I was doing.'

'Not too occupied to notice he was mauling you about and you didn't seem to be objecting,' he said coldly.

'Don't tell me you were jealous,' she said, smiling frostily.

He slid the window shut and then came and sat down on the sofa beside her, not touching her.

'Jealous—good God, no. Why should I be jealous? I merely felt responsible for you; that's why I came after you—as soon as I could get rid of Barbara.'

She clasped her hands tightly together to stop them shaking. 'Well, now you see I'm not being raped, perhaps you'll leave?'

He drew in a deep breath, as if asking for patience. 'You don't have to be like that, Anthea. You know there's nothing . . . personal between us. We agreed on that, didn't we?'

'I seem to remember something of the sort,' she said distantly. 'I merely thought that, as we were invited together this evening, your behaviour to me was rather rude. Which wouldn't be particularly unusual,' she added pointedly.

He groaned. 'Look, let's get this straight. I told you I had no intention of starting a holiday affair. You agreed that you didn't want one either. That was why——'

'Why you suggested using me so that your sister wouldn't annoy you by producing "nubile young girls"—wasn't that the term?—to heal your broken heart?'

'I didn't mean to "use" you,' he said gruffly. 'I certainly didn't look at it like that. I just thought— we seemed to get along pretty well, and it would be a good idea to . . . spend time together, that was all.'

'A lovely platonic friendship?'

'Something like that.'

'No tiny twinge of desire? No soupçon of lust?'

'Dammit, Anthea, you know there was. That was pretty evident on the beach this afternoon. I'm a man and you're a very attractive girl. What happened showed me the way *your* mind was working but it didn't change *my* mind—I'm not going to involve myself in a holiday liaison.' He got up and strode to the window and stood looking out at the dark, star-strewn sky. 'Why do you think I fooled around with that moronic girl Barbara this evening? To show you beyond doubt that I had no intention of accepting your flattering invitation. At the risk of sounding brutal, I must repeat what I think I told you at the beginning of our acquaintance—there's nothing doing, my dear girl. Nothing has changed.'

My dear girl! It was too much! The pompous—insufferable... She wouldn't let him get away with that—he had to be cut down to size. He was going to pay, she fumed, for making her feel cheap and humiliated.

The way was ready to hand, if only she could carry it off. She summoned a pathetically twisted little smile to her lips. 'But what would you say if I told you that something *has* changed, Charles? That *I've* changed? That I'm tired of playing the game by your rules? If I told you I love you?'

He stood very still for a moment. Then, violently, he swung round, and the look of consternation on his face was beautifully satisfying. She'd really got him worried now. He came back to sit beside her. 'No, you *don't*, Anthea. Of course you don't.' He took her hand in a hard grip that crushed her fingers. 'It's just the—the sun and the sea——' he waved an arm '—and the palm trees and the flowers...all the romantic clichés—they've got to you, that's all. In a week you'll have forgotten I ever existed.' His voice rose in his frantic effort to convince her. He was almost shouting.

Now was the time to play another card. She drew her hand away. 'I don't think I will,' she said, shaking her head sadly. 'You see, I've loved you for five years.'

'What?' he roared.

He stared at her incredulously, eyes wide, searching her face, dark brows drawn together in a frown. Then his mouth fell open almost comically. 'Good God! Now I remember. It was at a wedding party. You were wearing a pink dress and we stood on a balcony looking at the river—and you told me you were going to study design...'

In spite of her anger a wave of delight washed over her. He hadn't forgotten—not altogether.

'What happened to your career?' He seemed interested, but she was certain he was only changing the subject.

'Oh, I enjoyed my time at college,' she told him. 'Afterwards I worked in a fashion design studio. A friend of mine had a knitting machine she couldn't get the hang of and she lent it to me. I got interested in knitwear design. I began to sell some of the garments I made. After a while I gave up my job and started on my own—I managed to get a work-room in a disused factory in the East End.'

'Clever girl,' he said admiringly. 'Go on.'

'I was lucky, I suppose. Soon I was selling to the big stores and later on abroad. Paris, Rome—it was tremendously exciting.'

And then it was all over—everything gone up in smoke. But she wasn't going to tell him that. Sympathy was the last thing she wanted from him.

'So—you're in the big time, and you've done it all by yourself. I like that.' He gave her his most charming smile. He must be congratulating himself that he was tactfully steering the conversation out of dangerous channels. But she had more surprises in store for him.

'It wasn't quite all by myself,' she said, giving him a sideways glance under her long lashes. 'I had help—a guide and mentor.'

'Some man?'

Her mouth quirked. She was almost enjoying the game she was playing now. 'Is that surprising? I thought he was the most wonderful man in the world. He was everything that I admired in a man——' she gave a long, gusty sigh '—strong and kind and understanding—and sexy, of course. I kept his photograph pinned up on the wall and I used to talk to him and ask his advice and tell him all the stupid things that had gone wrong. It was—sort of comforting when I was working alone.'

'And when you'd finished work I suppose the fellow was even more—er—comforting?' he said drily.

She shook her head. 'We-ell—no. You see, he was only a pin-up—someone I adored from afar, like a pop star, or a film hero. I only met him once.' She looked down at her hands, a demure smile touching her lips. 'It was at a wedding party. I was wearing a pink dress and we stood on a balcony, looking at the river.' She heard his quick intake of breath and made a slight pause for effect and then continued, 'I didn't know anybody and I was feeling gauche and awkward

and he was kind to me. All the rest was a dream. I
don't think girls dream much about wonderful men
nowadays—or perhaps they still do—I don't know.
But I was very young and very silly.'

She stood up and walked across to the table, leaning
back against it, watching him, savouring her small
triumph. The room was suddenly quiet. Only the con-
tinuous chirping noise of the night insects found its
way through the closed window, and the distant
sighing of the waves.

Then she heard him draw in a harsh breath as the
whole truth dawned on him. He lifted his head and
there was a haggard expression on his face that took
her by surprise. 'Why didn't you tell me?' he said at
last, and his voice grated on her raw nerves. 'I'd never
for one moment have——'

'Walked into danger? Of course you wouldn't—
you'd have run like a hare,' she said lightly. 'If you
remember, I *did* tell you we'd met before and you
looked right through me as if I didn't exist. Then,
later on, at the tennis court you tried to annihilate
me. I suppose I was a bit peeved. So when you came
up with your grand scheme—*for your own convenience*—I thought it might be amusing to go along
with it. When you've built up a fantasy picture of
someone it's quite a temptation to find out how
right—or wrong—you are. And, my goodness, was I
wrong!'

His face hardened. He got up and stood in front
of her and said very quietly, 'And that kiss on the
beach this afternoon?'

'Oh—that!' She managed a laugh. 'I couldn't resist
finding out how close to my fantasy the reality was.'

'And . . .?' There was a dangerous note in his voice now, but she chose to ignore it. She was goading him, she knew it, and excitement pulsed through her.

She shrugged. 'Four out of ten, perhaps.'

His eyes narrowed and she shrank from the dark fury she saw in them. His arms went round her, squeezing the breath from her body. 'Then let's see if I can improve my score,' he ground out between his teeth, before his mouth came down on hers.

CHAPTER EIGHT

ANTHEA flapped her arms wildly, trying to push against his chest. But there was no space to get her hands between their two bodies. She was so sure that he would repeat his performance of this afternoon on the beach—when, for a few terrifying moments, he had lost control and turned savage—that she put all her strength into the effort to twist out of his grasp. Quite useless. She was clamped to him as surely as if he'd bound them together with steel wire.

His lips were pressed hard against hers and she waited helplessly for the punishment he was going to inflict on her. Instead, he raised his mouth a fraction and she saw his eyes, close and out of focus. They looked like pools of dark water, and she could almost imagine he was smiling.

'You little wretch,' he murmured. 'What am I going to do with you?'

She wriggled against him. 'Let me go—please let me——'

His mouth closed over the last word. His mouth—soft and warm and unexpectedly gentle. Anthea felt her knees buckle as the slow, exploratory movement of his tongue round her lips set up a painful ache inside her. Without taking his mouth away, he edged her towards the sofa and lowered her down on to it. It was a wide sofa—plenty of room for two, and Charles took full advantage of that, pinning her down by flinging one leg over both of hers. When she felt

126

his weight on her she gasped, 'No—no,' against his mouth.

'No what?' he mocked. 'You've had your fun, my sweet; now I'm going to have mine.'

Resting on one elbow, he rolled a little away and deftly undid the knot of the sash that held her filmy wrap closed. She grabbed at him as he pulled the fronts of the wrap apart, but he brushed her hand aside with the greatest of ease. Then she felt the cool air from the ceiling fan on her body, naked except for the lacy wisp of her panties. She heard his quick intake of breath. 'Lovely—much prettier without any covering.'

She was only too aware of the picture she must be presenting to him—her cheeks flushed, her breasts swelling, their peaks already hard and throbbing. A momentary consciousness of shame was swamped by the sensuous pleasure of being naked to the gaze of the man she loved.

Slowly, as if relishing the moment, he lowered his mouth to her breast and when his tongue stroked the nipples, one by one, her body jolted as if a powerful electric charge had been released into it. She sank back into the softness of the sofa, her head threshing on the cushion, moaning faintly as his lips closed tightly over one of the hard peaks, drawing it into his mouth. At the same time his hand was stroking her waist, moving over the rounded curves of her hips, her stomach, finding its way unerringly beneath the lacy bit of nothing that presented no barrier.

Wave after wave of heat ran through her as the exquisite torture went on. Nothing remotely like this had ever happened to her before. She had sometimes wondered what it would be like if he made love to her but that had been a thing of the imagination. This was real, entirely physical, every nerve contributing to the rising heat that burned through her.

She reached up and buried her fingers in the crisp hair at the nape of his neck, digging her nails convulsively into the damp skin there. She felt a deep shudder convulse him. Then, with a muttered curse, he rolled away from her and got to his feet, breathing fast. 'That's enough—more than enough,' he said roughly.

The shock of separation made her whimper. She felt a coldness, a loneliness, as if she had lost part of her own body. Then, slowly, she began to recover herself. She sat up, shivering, drawing the silk robe round her.

She felt his eyes on her but couldn't look up to meet them. She was burning with humiliation even while she shook with cold. All she wanted was to sink through the floor—to disappear completely. He had been calculating her response while she had been aroused to a point of frenzy. And he had known it, the brute; he had been watching her losing her mind, wallowing in passion, while he'd remained as unmoved as if he were—were tuning up a car engine.

He turned away and walked across the room, opening and closing doors in the built-in cupboard. She heard the noise of a cork's being pulled out, then he came back to her, holding out a tall glass. 'To cool you down,' he said, with a ghost of a smile.

The smile was the last straw. She took the glass, hurled the contents in his face, and threw the glass on the carpet. Then, to her utter mortification, she buried her head in the back of the sofa and burst into tears.

She covered her face with one hand, gulping and spluttering, while the other hand fumbled for the pocket in the gown she was wearing. In the pocket, by some merciful chance, was a wad of tissues. After she had choked away the tears she wiped her cheeks, dabbed her eyes and blew her nose hard. By then Charles would have left. There was no way he was going to stay and witness her abject performance. Men didn't have much patience with tears. She lifted her head cautiously to make sure he wasn't still there.

He was. He was leaning back in the easy chair next to the sofa, looking very much at home. He'd taken off his thin khaki shirt and it was lying in a sodden heap on the floor. In the subdued light from the reading lamp he looked bronzed and magnificent, the muscles rippling over his ribs and the dark shadow of hair streaking down to disappear at the belt of his jeans. I hate him, Anthea told herself. No, I don't, I'm crazy about him.

'Better now?' he enquired calmly.

She glared at him, saying nothing because she couldn't think of anything sufficiently hurtful to say.

'You know,' he went on calmly, 'I think we should call off the match at game-all. Another time, perhaps, we could play the deciding game of the set, but now's not the time.'

He leaned towards her, resting his forearms along his knees. 'Anthea, my dear,' he said urgently, 'let's not fight any more. Let's finish off the fortnight as friends—that way we'll have done something positive, however rocky it's been on the journey. I like you, I admire you tremendously. You're a lovely, warm, enchanting girl and if things had been different...'

He stopped, and for a moment the look of near-despair that she had seen before clouded his face. Then he brightened again. 'What do you say? Shall we call it quits?'

Let's finish the fortnight as friends. She pretended to consider it. She was starving and he was offering her a few crumbs of dry bread. He'd set her alight with his calculated lovemaking. What would it be like, she thought faintly, if it were real and not a sham? If he really wanted her as she wanted him? *Did he want her at all?* Or only when she made him angry? She remembered that time they had danced together on her first evening in the Caymans. He'd been angry then. And he'd certainly been angry on the beach this afternoon—angry with her for teasing him a little. Or had his response been nothing more than the act of a man desperately in need of a woman—any woman—who for a few moments could make him forget his real love—the unknown woman whose loss had poisoned his emotional life, leaving it barren and empty? She wished she knew.

'*Please*, Anthea.'

Two more days! Only one really, for tomorrow she would want to be with Pam when she got home. She wasn't sure that she could go on with the charade, not after all that had happened today. But if she refused it would be hideously difficult to explain to Nancy and to Pamela why they had quarrelled. If they parted as friends, when Charles left, the whole thing would just fade away and no questions asked—or not any that she couldn't tactfully evade.

She gave an almost imperceptible nod.

'Fine,' he said, treating her to a frank smile. 'No hard feelings? It's good to clear the air, don't you think?'

He'd got his own way—he was prepared to be charming. But *she* wasn't prepared to rake over any ashes. 'I'd like you to go now,' she said.

He got up immediately. 'Of course. How about tomorrow? You're expecting Pamela and Guy back, aren't you? Can I be of any assistance—take you to meet them perhaps?' he offered courteously.

'No, thank you,' she said, stiffly polite. 'They couldn't say which flight they'd be on so they'll get a taxi from the airport.'

'Ah, yes. Well, let me know if I can help. And we must try to fit in our final dive before I leave, mustn't we?'

'Perhaps—if there's time. I have to see how Pam is.'

'Yes, of course,' he agreed smoothly. 'Well, goodnight, Anthea.' He picked up his soggy khaki shirt and walked across the room. 'I expect we'll see each other some time tomorrow.' With a casual lift of his hand he departed the way he had come in—through the door on to the veranda.

Anthea leaned back and closed her eyes. That horrible, formal little exchange had left her feeling utterly deflated, like a burst balloon. She wasn't thinking; she wasn't really feeling either. She was just—empty.

After a time she got up and went to the kitchen for a cloth to dry the carpet as best as she could. She picked up the glass, which was unbroken, and carried it to the sink. Then she went upstairs to her bedroom. The moon had risen and the room was filled with white light and inky black shadows. After the heat of the day the air was blessedly cool with a little breeze wafting through the open window.

She stood beside the window, looking down to the sea where the moonlight threw squiggly ripples on the water. The endless stretch of sand gleamed silver as far as the eye could see. The palm trees sighed faintly and the cicadas put up their incessant shrill chirp. A perfect place, Anthea thought with detachment, but not the place to heal a broken heart. Charles hadn't managed it, and neither could she.

She closed the window and got into bed, lying on her back and staring at the ceiling. She'd go back to London as soon as she was reassured that Pamela didn't need her. The decision steadied her nerves. She felt a faint stir of enthusiasm for the task ahead— looking for a new work-room, getting started again on her designs, buying new machines. It was going to be a hard slog but she needed a demanding challenge if she was ever going to get Charles Ravenscroft out of her system.

She'd expected to lie awake for hours, but the decision to return to London had brought her a kind of peace and she fell asleep almost immediately.

The first thing Anthea heard when she wakened next morning was the hum of the vacuum downstairs. She pulled on her wrap and went down to find Juliana, wrapped in a red and white spotted apron, happily getting back into routine.

'My mother is better,' she told Anthea with her beautiful white smile. 'She tells me to go off to work again, so here I am. I give her half my wages, you see,' she added slyly.

Anthea laughed. 'I'm pleased to see you, Juliana. My sister and her husband are coming home today and I was going to do some cleaning myself. I'm afraid you'll find some dust around the place. I've been rather lazy.'

'Not lazy at all!' Juliana shook her dark head vehemently. 'You come for holiday, not to work yourself to frazzle. You have a good holiday?'

'Oh, yes, marvellous,' Anthea said, putting an ecstatic smile on her mouth. 'Who wouldn't in this heavenly place?'

Juliana nodded. 'I see you around with Mr Charles from next door.' She nodded sagely. 'Very good-looking man, that one!' The sloe-black eyes slid knowingly towards Anthea's.

'Yes—well—I'll go up and get dressed,' Anthea said hastily and escaped to her bedroom. Juliana worked for Nancy too, and no doubt would be asking some loaded questions when she got there. There was a villagey atmosphere in the condo and Juliana probably considered herself part of it.

By one o'clock the apartment was clean and polished, flowers were massed in every reasonably cool corner, and between them Anthea and Juliana had prepared a special native dish of conch and lobster which could stay in the fridge until required for supper.

'You like me to make you some lunch before I go?' Juliana offered, but Anthea thanked her and declined. She wasn't really hungry; perhaps being 'crossed in love' really did take your appetite away. Coffee was always welcome though, and when Juliana had left for her afternoon stint next door Anthea made coffee in Pamela's gleaming percolator and carried it out to the table on the veranda.

Five minutes later Nancy's head appeared round the woven grass screen that partly separated the two sections of the veranda. 'Do I smell coffee?'

'You certainly do. Come and join me—I'll get an extra mug.' Anthea welcomed her neighbour with pleasure.

During the time Pamela had been away Anthea had grown very fond of Charles's sister. Her apparent bluntness was actually an inability to put on an act. Her fussiness was a practical desire to help. She was a 'real' person, Anthea recognised, and there were all too few of them about. She understood, now, why Charles had jibbed against hurting her feelings when she had ingenuously tried to matchmake on his behalf. But understanding didn't help to make her feel any less guilty and uneasy about her own part in his little charade.

Nancy sank into a cane chair. She was wearing a brightly patterned sun-dress and she radiated good sense and good humour.

'Phew! I had to get away from Juliana; she makes me feel weak the way she buzzes round at ninety miles an hour. And talk! She talks the hind leg off a donkey, as my old granny used to say. Thanks, dear...' as Anthea passed a mug of coffee across the table. 'She likes to know everything that's happening to "her" folks—as she thinks of us, here in the condo. She's a good soul but it gets a bit much sometimes. This morning she wanted to know...' She paused and threw an apologetic glance towards Anthea. 'No—I mustn't embarrass you; I expect you can guess what I was going to say.'

Anthea sipped her coffee with a fair attempt at nonchalance. 'Yes, she was throwing hints around when she was here. She'd seen me with Charles, apparently. "Very good-looking man, that one."' She mimicked the girl's faint lilt with a grin.

Nancy sighed. 'Yes, I must say I agree, although he *is* my brother.' She was silent for a time and Anthea cast around desperately for something to say that would change the subject. But before she could think of anything, Nancy burst out impulsively, 'I've been worried about him, Anthea; I think you know that. Poor boy, he's been going through a very bad patch. A woman, of course—isn't it always some woman?' Her squarish good-natured face was suddenly venomous. 'Oh, she was beautiful, of course. The face of an angel and a heart of pure steel. The kind of woman that even the most intelligent of men make fools of themselves over.'

Nancy had been gripping her coffee-mug as if she would have liked to grip the neck of this unknown beauty who had ensnared her beloved brother. Now she put the mug down, her lips twisting apologetically. 'I expect you think I'm behaving like a possessive mama, but since we lost our parents when Charles was ten and I six years older—they were drowned in a sailing accident in Australia—I've felt a kind of...responsibility. Silly, I suppose, now we're both grown up, but when I think what Charles was like before that——' her mouth narrowed '—before that bitch Elsa got her claws into him, and the way it left him when it was all over, it makes me see red. Sometimes I was afraid...'

Suddenly the brown eyes were flooded with tears. Nancy sniffed and blew her nose. 'Sorry—I'm not usually a cry-baby. I don't know why I'm inflicting all this on you, my dear, except that you've been so good for Charles. He's gradually become more like his old self since he's known you. I shouldn't interfere, I know, but I must say it—you're so right for him. It's a shame he has to go back to London on Friday—a board meeting or something. But you'll be leaving for London yourself before very long?' she added hopefully. 'I expect you'll be meeting up there.'

'Maybe we shall,' Anthea said carefully. It was hateful having to deceive Nancy, for that was what it amounted to, but when Charles was back in London and Nancy was here in the Caymans this fortnight would fade into the past quite rapidly. Charles would get over his hurt in time and no doubt find another girl. But it wouldn't be *her*. Sadly she thought that she had come across him again at the worst possible time. Perhaps if they'd met later, when the wound had healed, perhaps... But that sort of thinking led nowhere. The time was now, and two weeks hadn't been long enough. The wound was still too raw for him to turn to a new love.

Nancy got to her feet. 'I'll be off, then. I'm getting the bus into town to meet Bill for lunch. Charles has gone out in the dive-boat with Joe this morning. I'll look forward to seeing Pamela—tomorrow, perhaps, when she's rested after the journey. Give her my love. Thanks for the coffee.'

She gave Anthea a faintly embarrassed smile. Probably she was regretting having lowered her guard, Anthea thought, watching the compact figure disappear round the grass screen. In spite of her friendly, open approach, there was a dignity, a strength about Nancy that didn't show on the surface.

When she had gone Anthea stayed sitting on the veranda, leaning her head back, her eyes closed against the bright sunlight that filtered through the canopy, thinking of what Nancy had told her about Charles. How little she knew of him! Their fortnight together had been such a strange time. Normally, a man and a girl getting to know each other would ask so many questions. Every little detail would be of vital interest. But Charles had been absolutely unapproachable. All she knew of him she'd just learned from Nancy: that they had lived in Australia when he was a boy; that their parents had been drowned; that he'd had a passionate love-affair with a girl called Elsa, which seemed to have wrecked his life. 'The kind of woman that...men make fools of themselves over.' Yes, it was all quite clear now; everything was clear, and she had never stood a chance with him.

The sun had attained its maximum heat and she felt the sweat breaking out on her forehead. The effort of trying to be sensible about everything had left her feeling nervy and unsettled. She must find something to do.

On an impulse she went back inside and rang up the airport to enquire the time of arrival of the next flight from Miami. Learning that it was due in just under half an hour, she phoned for a taxi. She'd meet the plane on the off-chance that Pamela and Guy would be on it.

She hadn't long to wait. In the arrivals hall she watched eagerly as the first passengers began to dribble through from Customs. Americans, bright as proverbial buttons, talking thirteen to the dozen, Europeans looking distinctly weary, with a long flight behind them. They came in couples, in parties, some

looking around for taxis, others for friends expected
to meet them.

Anthea's spirits drooped with disappointment as the
crowd of arrivals began to thin out, with no sign of
Pamela and Guy. The buzz of greetings faded as the
lounge emptied. The last few stragglers emerged. A
couple speaking German, with two exhausted-looking
small boys. Two middle-aged ladies determinedly
pushing trolleys. And then, walking alone and
carrying only a weekend briefcase, a young woman
who caught Anthea's eye immediately because of the
contrast she presented with the crowd of holiday-
makers.

Anthea's glance passed over the reed-thin figure in
its black silk suit—which looked hideously expensive
but quite unsuitable for arrival at a holiday hotel. One
of the new breed of female business tycoons probably,
Anthea thought without much interest. Then she
caught a glimpse of the girl's face and felt a small
shock. It was a beautiful face, a perfect oval, but in
spite of the careful make-up the skin seemed pallid
and the huge smoke-grey eyes stared straight ahead
with an oddly haunted look. Even when she had
passed, the memory of those strange eyes remained
with Anthea as she waited with dwindling hope for
Pamela and her husband to emerge, until there wasn't
any point in waiting longer.

At the information office she was told that the only
other flight from Miami was due to arrive at nine-
thirty tonight. She calculated quickly. Another seven
wasted hours when she might have been with Charles.
She felt terrible. She should be thinking about Pam;
instead she was trying to face the rest of her life

without Charles and seeing only a long black tunnel of days.

Despondently she went back to the taxi she had booked to wait. 'Bribed' might have been a better word, because she had given the driver a hefty tip to ensure his compliance, in case Pamela was on the flight.

The taxi was still there on the forecourt—the only one remaining—and the girl in black was standing beside it, conducting a one-sided argument with the driver, who was leaning back, chewing gum and regarding her without much interest.

'Well, when will there be another cab?' Her voice was high-pitched and nervous and not at all in character with her sleek, groomed appearance.

Anthea approached the taxi and the driver reached out and opened the passenger door for her.

She smiled at him and turned to the girl. 'Like to share a cab into town? It's maddening to be left high and dry.'

'Thanks,' the girl muttered and climbed into the taxi.

Anthea followed and sat beside her. 'Where shall I tell him? I'm going beyond the town myself.'

'Oh—oh, anywhere.' Anthea noticed that her voice was unsteady and the white hands clasping her briefcase shook slightly.

The taxi trundled along the dusty road towards George Town. Anthea glanced at the girl beside her. She really was exquisite, her hair glossy as a raven's wing, her skin so fine and white and perfect, and those enormous grey eyes that Anthea had first noticed staring straight ahead with a fixed gaze.

They couldn't just sit here saying nothing. 'I came to meet my sister and her husband,' she said pleasantly, 'but they must have missed the plane.'

'Oh,' murmured the girl indifferently.

'You here on holiday?' Anthea tried.

The great grey eyes met hers and she experienced an odd shock. They were swimming in tears. The girl shook her head, swallowed back the tears and turned away again.

One didn't intrude on a stranger's troubles. There was silence until the taxi reached the town.

Anthea leaned forward. 'Please stop at the harbour,' she told the driver, and to the girl, 'You can reach most places from there. Will that suit you?'

The girl nodded wordlessly. When the car pulled up she fumbled in her bag, but Anthea touched her hand. It was icy cold. 'Please don't,' she said. 'I have to go on further in any case.'

'Thanks, then.' The girl climbed out and stood looking around uncertainly as the taxi moved away.

The driver turned his head with a smile. 'You goin' back home, miss?'

'Yes, please.' Anthea wondered briefly about the girl they had just left. But you couldn't worry long about strangers' troubles when you had plenty of your own.

At the condo she paid the driver and walked slowly from the car park. As she went she counted the hours that were left. 'I'll see you tomorrow,' Charles had said. And, 'We must . . . fit in our final dive before I leave.'

But Charles wasn't around today and now it looked as if she might not have any free time tomorrow. There was no way she could go off with Charles when

Pamela had just come home—even if he asked her to. Perhaps, she thought bleakly, it would be better that way, better that they wouldn't be alone together again. Their fortnight would end—fizzle out miserably. She felt black gloom settling round her, blotting out the sunshine.

Then she turned the corner and saw him coming to meet her and felt a sharp painful twinge behind her ribs.

'Where have you been? I've been waiting for you.' He took her arm and led her to the veranda. 'You OK? You look fagged.'

She sank into a chair. 'I'm fine—just hot. I've been to the airport to meet Pam and Guy but they weren't on the plane.'

'That's what I guessed. I've got a message for you. Pamela and Guy aren't coming back until tomorrow. Guy tried to ring you here and when there wasn't any reply he got through to our number. Nancy's out so I took the message. It's OK——' as Anthea shot up in her chair, eyes widening with alarm '—everything's fine. Pamela spoke to me herself.'

She relaxed with a sigh of relief, fanning her hot cheeks with her hand.

'You need a drink,' Charles said. 'Look, let me find something in Guy's drinks cupboard for you. What'll you have?'

'Something long and cool, please.' She watched him as he made for the door into the living-room. How brown his legs were, the dark hairs almost invisible against the skin, and how wide his shoulders under the white cotton vest! She thought in sudden panic, Oh, God, I love him. How am I going to live when he's gone?

'Here you are.' He put a tall glass into her hand as he sat down beside her. A grin touched the corners of his mouth. 'And for Pete's sake *drink* it this time, and don't hurl it in my face.'

She took a gulp of the ice-cold fruity drink. 'I'm sorry,' she muttered.

The grin turned into a laugh—a hearty guffaw. 'Don't let's start swapping apologies again—we'll never get to the end.' He peered down into her face. 'You *are* looking bushed. When did you last eat?'

She blinked foolishly. 'I had breakfast—I think.'

'Breakfast, you *think*!' he roared. 'And it's half-past three now. Don't you know you shouldn't skip meals just because you're in the tropics? And you're probably dehydrated too. Go on, finish your drink while I rustle up a sandwich for you.'

He got to his feet. 'As things have turned out we've got the rest of today to ourselves. Nancy and Bill won't be in until later, so we can make plans. We'll pick up our gear at Joe's, hire one of his inflatables and take it out beyond the reef. We can get into fairly deep water there—find a good drop-off. Diving from a boat's the one thing I haven't taught you. We must make our last dive together really memorable.'

She gave a mock shiver. 'You sound like the condemned man planning to eat a hearty breakfast.'

Suddenly the bleak, haggard look that she was beginning to recognise swept over his face. 'Don't say things like that,' he said sharply. He rested one hand on the table and the dark, sombre eyes stared down into hers. She could almost imagine he was memorising her face, but that was wishful thinking of course.

He straightened up. The moment was past. He said briskly, 'OK, you go and get changed. I'll raid the fridge and you can eat in the car. That way we won't waste any time.'

Anthea went upstairs, slipped quickly into the businesslike white swim-suit she wore for diving, and pulled a blue cover-up over it. There was a feeling of urgency now; she was no longer counting the days but the hours. Everything they did together would be for the last time so she must savour every minute. She mustn't allow herself to think of what would come after he had gone.

She peered in the mirror. Smile, she ordered sternly. Go on, smile.

It wasn't easy but she managed it, and before the smile faded from her lips she ran lightly downstairs to join Charles.

CHAPTER NINE

'WE'LL anchor here.' Charles switched off the engine and the small rubber dinghy rocked very gently in the water. He peered over the side. 'Should go down to twenty metres here—quite deep enough for a raw beginner.' He smiled lazily across at Anthea.

He was in his friendly, teasing mood. She liked that. This last time together must be happy—something to remember for years, perhaps forever.

She looked all around, trying to stack away every detail: the changing colours of the water from brilliant sapphire here beyond the line of the reef to glassy turquoise nearer the beach; a few dinghies with rainbow-striped sails; a white yacht moored offshore; a figure, dangling from a red and yellow parachute rising out of the water on a tow-line. The long strip of white sand was almost empty. At this time in the afternoon most of the visitors would be found lounging round their pools in the low-built hotels and clubs and condominiums that nestled behind the row of palm trees along the whole length of Seven Mile Beach. It was very quiet. The occasional scream of a seabird and the putt-putting of an outboard motor seemed to come from a long way away.

Out here, beyond the reef, there was only the smell of heat and sea and rubber, the silvery dazzle of sun on water—and Charles sitting across the boat from her, eyes narrowed against the sun, teeth white against bronzed cheeks. He looked so happy—he always did

144

when he was on a diving expedition. Oh, God, I love him, she thought, and her heart squeezed up inside her.

She tipped her head back. 'Am I still a raw beginner? I thought I was making spectacular progress.'

He pursed his lips. 'I don't like the word spectacular. It has a hectic sound about it. Diving should be relaxed always, and over-confidence is the greatest hazard.'

'Oh,' breathed Anthea, feeling rather dashed.

'Having said which——' Charles smiled '—you are probably the best pupil I've ever had. You do what you're told, you don't jib at getting down to the sometimes boring theory. And you learn so quickly I'm positively amazed at how much you've remembered.'

Anthea chuckled. 'Thank you for those kind words.' She wouldn't tell him how many hours she had spent in bed poring over a book of Guy's she had found on scuba diving.

'And——' he continued, '—you're looking particularly lovely today, Anthea. You have five freckles on your delightful nose.'

She was glad the light was so strong that he wouldn't notice her blush.

'Now.' He was all businesslike again as he paid out the anchor-line. 'I've planned the dive—times and everything. You can leave that part to me. You know the underwater drill. Entering from the boat is the only new thing. I go first and wait for you on the surface. You sit on the tubes, check the water behind you, hold one hand over mask and demand valve, the other on the cylinder harness, tuck your head forwards. Relax and roll backwards over the side. You'll

bob up like a cork immediately. Signal OK to me and
then we duck-dive together to get underwater, turn,
and drop feet first. Remember to clear your ears as
we go, and to breathe easily. Any questions?'

'No—sir,' she grinned.

'Am I a hard taskmaster, Anthea?' He met her eyes
quizzically.

'We-ell,' she drawled, looking up questioningly into
the pale blue of the sky. 'Let's just say——' she looked
down again, '—the best. The very best.'

For a moment she thought he seemed taken aback.
Had she given herself away—had she let the love she
felt for him shine out of her eyes? Oh, please not, she
thought; that would spoil everything. Friends they
were—'buddies' in diving parlance—and friends they
must remain until the end. That way there would be
no room for bitterness or recriminations. 'Do we get
ourselves kitted up now?' she asked practically,
reaching for her pile of neatly stacked gear on the
bottom of the boat.

Afterwards she was to remember how perfectly
everything went at first—probably because she had
absolute trust in Charles and obeyed his orders in
every smallest detail. There was something wonderful
and strange about dropping slowly hand-in-hand
through crystal-clear water, bubbles rising above them
to the sunlit surface, clouds of tiny coloured fish con-
tinually changing direction around them with a swish
of a hundred tails.

And on the sea-bed there was the marvellous array
of coral and sponges, brown and blue and gold, the
waving green feathers of plants, the larger, lazier fish,
that sometimes formed an interested audience, peering
into their masks.

At this depth the light became dim and mysterious, but the visibility was still so good on the sea-bed that Charles now and then loosed his hold and allowed Anthea to roam free, although keeping very close. She finned in a sort of ecstatic trance, exploring, touching, encountering fish that she hadn't seen on their dives in shallower water. Many of them seemed quite tame. At one point she met a particularly friendly blue and gold angel fish which followed her like a pet dog waiting to be stroked. Anthea looked for Charles to share her delight with him.

That was when everything began to go wrong. He was about six feet away from her and as she signed to him to come closer she saw that he was signing back to her. Not the usual finger and thumb sign of 'OK', but the distress signal. Clenched fists waving to and fro urgently, then his cupped hand pointing to his mouthpiece.

The signal that meant, 'Out of air, assistance required immediately.'

For a split second icy terror ran through Anthea's every nerve. Then, immediately, she was completely calm. They had practised emergency ascents together during sessions in shallow water. But this wasn't a practice session, this was for real, and they were in deep water. If he'd been going to risk a free ascent he would have started up immediately. But he was waiting for her. He was relying on her help. His life depended on her.

Those thoughts flashed through her head in the time it took to reach him, to set in motion the drill that she had learned. Then some strength outside herself took over. She was cool, confident, automatic. Not a thought entered her head except those that told her exactly what she had to do.

Taking in two good breaths as she moved towards Charles, she grasped the strap of his harness, removed her mouthpiece and held it out to him with the air flowing. He took hold of one strap of her harness so that they were facing, and with the other hand guided the mouthpiece into his own mouth.

As he drew in several life-saving breaths she sent up a prayer of thanksgiving. It worked! She exhaled gently until he handed the mouthpiece back to her.

After a steady breathing-and-exchange rhythm was established she saw that Charles was in control again. 'Going up,' he signalled, and she replied with the 'OK' signal.

Face to face, holding each other by their harnesses, they rose steadily at the rate of the small bubbles above them, carrying out faithfully the one decompression stop which Charles had planned. Finally they were on the surface and she was drawing in wonderful, life-giving air, and the inflatable boat was only about ten metres away.

Anthea could never remember swimming to the boat or how she managed to pull herself in when she reached it.

The next thing she knew was that her harness and fins had been removed and she was sprawled on the bottom, that Charles had started the motor, and they were heading towards the land.

After that everything was hazy. She had done what she had to do and now shock was taking its toll. She was dimly aware of Charles's helping her out into shallow water and then of them both dragging the boat the last few yards on to the sand.

She was feeling very odd now, her body heavy as lead. But she mustn't give in. Charles was the one who might have drowned down there—she mustn't be the one to falter now. 'Shall I carry...?' she began, and suddenly keeled over on to the warm sand.

Charles was towering above her. 'I'll do the carrying round here,' he said, and picked her up easily.

It was so heavenly in his arms. She snuggled against him as he strode up the beach to the condo. How had they got here? she thought stupidly. They'd taken the boat out from the slipway outside the dive-shop. But it wasn't important. She turned her head a little into the damp warmth of his neck. His skin smelled delicious. She touched it delicately with her tongue and the salt burned her mouth.

He carried her straight upstairs, and lowered her on to the bed. She found she was shivering, which was absurd when it was stiflingly hot in the bedroom.

'Now you're going to rest,' Charles said. 'Let's get this swim-suit off.' He slipped the straps over her shoulders and, gripping the clinging stretch-fabric, began to ease it down.

'I can do it,' she gasped, trying to swing her legs to the floor.

'Lie down,' he ordered firmly, 'and don't be silly.' He pushed her back and gave the swim-suit one last tug. She felt it slipping over her stomach, her thighs, her legs.

'*That's* better.' He dropped the swim-suit on the floor and covered her with the duvet. 'Now you relax and don't dare to move. I'll go and make some nice hot tea. Always good recovery drill after the shock and tension of an emergency.' The dark eyes were looking down at her with—could it be tenderness? Or was she just imagining it?

'But—but what about you?' she stammered. 'It wasn't just me having the emergency—I feel such an idiot, flaking out like this.'

'Shut up, darling,' he said gently, and went out of the room.

She closed her eyes. He'd called her 'darling', and looked at her as if—as if...

By the time he came back with tea on a tray the shivering had stopped and she felt almost normal. Charles put the tray down and indicated his navy swimming trunks, which had a large slit up one side. 'Must have snagged them climbing into the boat. Do you think Guy would lend me some clobber? I don't want to risk going in next door in case Nancy's back and I have to start explaining.'

'Of course—help yourself. It's the room next to the bathroom.'

She would have to get something to cover herself. She couldn't sit up in bed to drink her tea showing her naked top half, and to pull up the duvet as protection would look ridiculous—especially as Charles had already seen all there was to see of her when he'd removed her swim-suit.

She slid out of bed and staggered towards the wardrobe. But her knees felt like elastic and she had to steady herself against the dressing-table, breathing hard.

'What are you doing? I told you to stay put.' Charles came up behind her and grabbed her round the waist. He had put on a pair of Guy's linen trousers and the stiffened material rubbed against her bare hips.

'I—I wanted to get my robe.' She nodded towards the wardrobe.

'I'll get it,' he said but didn't make any move, and his arm crept further round her waist until it rested under the swell of her breast. 'Nice,' he murmured and buried his mouth in the nape of her neck. She felt his tongue licking the skin below her hair, and her heart did a somersault.

'Salty—I like plenty of salt on my food,' he chuckled.

He was playing it light, so she must do the same. 'Too much salt's bad for you, didn't you know? Raises your blood-pressure.'

Suddenly he twisted her round until she was facing him. 'I don't need salt to do that,' he said softly and drew her against him, kissing her very gently.

'Charles—oh, Charles. I thought you were going to die!' She flung her arms round his neck and kissed him back with growing frenzy, pressing her body against his, thrilling to the growing hardness she encountered there. She was in his arms, where she wanted to be, and for a few mad moments she was going to forget the rules he'd made.

She felt him start to draw away and she clung even tighter. 'No,' he said shakily. 'It's not on, darling.'

'It is, oh, it *is*,' she pleaded. She'd never felt like this before—wanton and soft and swelling, and aflame with the intensity of a passion that had been growing and growing for all the days they'd spent together. Like a strong plant, pushing up out of the ground towards the sunlight.

Somehow they were lying on the bed and she could feel him trembling against her. 'It won't do,' he groaned. 'God, I want you too, my darling, but I've nothing to offer you. Nothing. *Nothing.*'

'It doesn't matter,' she sobbed. 'I don't care—I'd have a memory. Oh, *please*, Charles.'

She heard him mutter something that sounded like 'forgive', and then he was dragging feverishly at the zip of his trousers and his weight was on her and they were together, naked.

Once his control had finally broken he took all he wanted from her with hands and mouth, exploring every part of her eager body, every mound, every crevice, raising her to a point of frenzy where she writhed beneath him, her nails digging into the taut muscles of his shoulders, whimpering with a rising tension that was pain as well as pleasure. When he plunged into her she arched against him in a fierce response, holding her breath, moving with him in a wild climb to some undreamed-of peak, moaning in ecstasy as they reached that peak together and he gave a strangled, harsh cry and shuddered against her in an explosive consummation that made the bed rock beneath them.

It was over. That was Anthea's first coherent thought as he rolled off her and lay, panting, on the edge of the bed. It was over and it wouldn't happen again. It was as though she were hearing the tolling of a funeral bell. A choking sound that wasn't quite a laugh escaped her. Funny to compare what had just happened to a funeral.

Beside her, Charles muttered, 'Game, set and match—is that what you're thinking?'

She turned her head on the pillow and let her eyes feast on his face. Under the tan there was a flush high on his cheekbones. A lock of dark hair fell raggedly over his forehead and she stretched out and pushed it back gently, letting her hand linger on the damp, hot skin. 'It was you who turned it into a game, remember? But if it means I've won, then I suppose I should feel triumphant.'

'And you don't?' He grasped her hand and put it to his lips. 'What *do* you feel?'

She smiled dreamily. 'Satisfied. Replete. Sad.'

'Not regretful?'

'No, not regretful. If I won the match it was only because I cheated and broke the rules you'd laid down at the start. But I'm not sorry.'

There was a long pause. Then he swivelled round, his back to her, thrusting his legs into Guy's trousers. 'I've got to ask you this, Anthea. You took me by surprise when we were both—disturbed by what had just happened out there.' He gestured towards the window. 'Is it possible that you might have got yourself pregnant?'

She drew in a quick breath. He had hurt her so often that one more hurt didn't really matter. 'No, it isn't possible,' she said evenly, and heard his sigh of relief. She managed a small laugh. 'A girl doesn't come for a holiday on a tropical holiday island without some—protection.'

The look he gave her might have been ironic—she hoped it wasn't. 'So you *were* hoping for a holiday affair, with the usual trimmings. You told me——'

She sat up quickly, then realised she was still naked and made a quick dash for the wardrobe. Struggling into jeans and a cotton top, she said angrily, 'I was *not* hoping for a holiday affair. Sex was the last thing on my mind until...'

'Until?' he prompted quietly.

'Until I met my dream hero again.' She managed a silly little giggle. 'It was all *so* romantic. Just like in the novels.'

He crossed the room in a couple of strides and took her by both shoulders. As he studied her face she felt her smile fading under the scrutiny of those sombre black eyes.

'Was that all it was? Was it, Anthea?' He gave her a little shake. 'I want the truth.'

Their eyes locked and held. She said slowly, 'If you'd died down there, I shouldn't have wanted to go on living. I know it won't alter anything, but I may as well tell you.'

'Tell me—what?'

'That I love you,' she said simply.

She wriggled away from him. 'Look, the tea's gone cold,' she said in a high, brittle voice. 'How about that for a botched recovery drill? I'll go down and make some more; I think we both need it.'

Down in the kitchen she put the kettle on and stood leaning against the sink. She felt weak and shaky and she didn't know how she was going to face Charles again. For minutes there was no sound upstairs and then, just as the kettle boiled, she heard him coming down. He didn't join her in the kitchen and for a blank moment she wondered if he had walked straight out of the apartment, frightened out of his wits by her avowal of love.

But when she carried the tray into the living-room he was there, sitting on a corner of the sofa. He was wearing one of Guy's shirts—a short-sleeved cotton in a burnt orange colour.

'Very fetching! Just your colour!' Her mouth felt stiff but she managed a small smile.

He jumped up and took the tray from her, and she sat down in a chair by the window.

'Not there—here.' He put down the tray and gripped both her hands, pulling her up to sit beside him on the sofa. 'Your hands are cold,' he said. 'And this time you're going to drink the tea. You need it.' He poured out a cup and handed it to her, watching while she took a long gulp.

'That's better.' He followed suit, and between them they drank the pot dry. Anthea began to feel warm again, confidence creeping back to stiffen her spine. He'd asked for the truth and she'd given it to him, that was all. She didn't expect him to make any sudden U-turn, but there was no doubt that in the last half-hour things had changed between them. Colour crept into her cheeks as she remembered some of the ways they had changed.

He pushed the low table away and leaned back, not touching her. 'Now,' he said, 'we've carried out the proper recovery drill. Hot tea and relaxation. Especially relaxation.' He slid her an amused glance and her spirits shot up. He wasn't going to be stiff and awkward about her confession of love. He probably thought that she had been persuading herself that she was the kind of girl who wouldn't sleep with a man unless she'd convinced herself that she loved him. Oh, damn! It was all so complicated.

'I haven't thanked you,' he went on. 'I suppose you know that you may have saved my life.'

'I did what you taught me.' She made herself ask the question, 'What would have happened if I'd got it wrong?'

'I'd have made a free ascent. But from that depth it would have been—unpleasant.'

'And risky?'

He shrugged. 'Yes.'

She shivered, remembering that first moment of panic. She said, 'You sound so—sort of cool about it all. Weren't you even a bit scared?' Perhaps if she could break through the defensive wall he'd set up round himself—if she could get him to admit to an ordinary human frailty such as fear—perhaps then he'd unburden himself even more.

'Scared? The first moment when I breathed in and there was nothing there I was petrified. But I've been diving for a long time, Anthea, and accidents do sometimes happen. It helps to know what you have to do. I had to decide in a split second whether to start a free ascent straight away, or whether to wait and lose valuable time, trusting that you'd keep your head. I trusted—and you did. It was your first emergency and you handled it like a pro.' He smiled at her— a smile that seemed to trickle all over her body, warming every part of it.

His praise was very sweet to her, but not a single brick of the defences had loosened.

She swallowed a sigh. 'What went wrong—do you know?'

He shook his head. 'I'll have to examine the gear to find out. But——' he frowned to himself '—I have a horrible feeling that the fault was mine. I may not have checked my contents gauge carefully enough. Quite unforgivable if that's the case.' His mouth set in a grim line. 'In this game one can't afford to let one's concentration slip—whatever the excuse.'

He was looking at her as if she was in some way responsible, which was absurd, of course. In other circumstances that remark might have been flirtatious, but not now, and certainly not from Charles!

'Perhaps you'll find a fault in the equipment,' she said rather stiffly.

'Perhaps.' He stood up. 'Now, I'll go down and rescue the dinghy and take it back to Joe's. I can check in all the hired stuff—yours and mine. I shan't dive tomorrow—not without my "buddy"——' he slanted a quick grin at her which melted her brief annoyance '—and I'll be leaving early Friday morning. What shall I tell Joe about your hired gear? Will you be staying on?'

'I don't know—it depends on how Pamela is when she gets home tomorrow, and whether she needs me to stay longer. But I certainly won't be diving again. In any case, I'd have to be careful to leave a safe interval before flying, wouldn't I?'

There was something horribly final about this conversation. Everything was being tidied up, like shiny crumpled paper after a Christmas party. Tidied up and thrown away. No past—no future, he'd said. He'd made love to her because she had almost forced herself on him. No doubt he'd enjoyed it—certainly he'd appeared to—but, man-like, he would soon have forgotten all about it, and about her.

She got to her feet beside him. She felt more in control of herself when she was standing up. There was something she had to say and she couldn't think of the right words.

Finally she blurted out, 'It's the end of our fortnight and I want to...'

He took a step towards her and touched her mouth with his palm. 'No farewell speeches,' he said. 'You haven't got rid of me yet. Where would you like to go for dinner? Shall we dine in—or out? If it's up to me to decide I'd vote for eating here—am I invited?'

Reprieve—if only for a few hours! She wanted to dance and sing. Instead she dropped a mock curtsy. 'I should be honoured.'

'Good.' He lingered at the door. 'Anthea . . .'

'Yes?' She held her breath. There was something in his face; was the defensive wall cracking—ever so slightly?

'I—there are things I must tell you. I owe it to you,' he said bleakly. 'Later,' he added, and went out through the door on to the veranda.

She watched him run down the beach and push out the dinghy. She could almost sense the dammed-up energy in him as he heaved himself over the side and started up the motor. The dinghy headed out to sea and then turned sharply towards the south end of the beach, where Joe's shop was located. Charles raised a hand as if he knew she might be still there, watching. She waved back, although by now she would be out of sight to him.

She leaned against the window frame. She still had a few hours left. Dinner for two. Wine, candles, moonlight, the scent of flowers drifting in through the window, music—all the old romantic trappings. And why not, if it helped to get under his defences?

There was a skip in her step as she made her way to the kitchen to set about preparing a meal.

It was more than an hour before he came back. The meal was all ready in the kitchen—the conch and lobster dish prepared this morning, salad crisping in the fridge, a luscious-looking fruity concoction that Juliana had brought with her from one of the

specialist shops in the town, crusty rolls and butter.
Charles could choose the wine himself from Guy's
store.

Anthea fussed round the table in the living-room,
flicking an imaginary crumb off the snowy cloth, re-
polishing the immaculately gleaming silver, touching
the little posy of pink and white flowers she had
gathered from the shrubs in the garden. Nature was
co-operating by laying on a spectacular sunset. Outside
the window the sky and sea were merged in a blaze
of rose and apricot and salmon with streaks of palest
sea-green and wispy veils of silvery grey.

She heard the sound of a car and her heart began
to thud against her ribs. It might be Nancy and Bill
coming home of course, but . . .

Charles's step sounded on the veranda and his size
almost blotted out the sunset as he appeared at the
window.

Looking at him, she was beset by an awful shyness.
'Hello, you're back,' she said, smiling foolishly.

He was smiling too, but his smile wasn't foolish at
all; it was definitely purposeful. He came straight to
her and took her in his arms and kissed her with
lingering satisfaction. Immediately she knew that
something had changed. The wall between them was
coming down. When he lifted his mouth he held her
away and looked down into her face. ' "Anthea, Who
May Command Him Anything",' he quoted softly.

She swallowed past a huge lump in her throat. She
couldn't believe that this was happening—there was
a dream-like quality about it. But she mustn't take
more for granted than he intended to imply. She
looked up at him under her lashes. 'Is that true? Very
well, then, how about starting by choosing a wine for

us? Over there, slave.' She indicated the drinks
cupboard.

He made a mock obeisance and crossed the room
as she went into the kitchen. 'White or red?' he called
through the doorway.

'What do you think? It's a fishy concoction with
salad. That's all there was time for.' She wheeled the
trolley in.

'Mm—looks delicious. White would be à la mode,
I suppose, but I think we'll forget about being correct.
Guy's got a very nice-looking *rosé* here. OK?'

'OK.' The smile seemed to be fixed on her mouth.
She *hadn't* been imagining it before—the atmosphere
between them had changed completely, become almost
intimate. There was something satisfyingly domestic
in the way Charles hunted for a gadget to remove the
cork, in the way he drifted out to the kitchen to help
her bring in the salad and mayonnaise and butter from
the fridge, and sawed hunks from the crusty loaf. In
the way he settled down at the table with an appreci-
ative, 'Well, this is nice.'

'I looked in next door,' he told her, when they had
helped themselves. 'Nancy and Bill are just back. I
told them they could find me here if they wanted me—
but I didn't encourage them to want me.' The grin he
slipped to her was a promise and her heart missed a
beat.

She said, 'What did Joe think—about . . .'

'About our slight contretemps?' His mouth twisted.
'Oh, Joe's a realist. So long as nobody needed urgent
treatment for the bends—you know, decompression
sickness—he didn't ask too many questions. But he
knows—and he knows that I know—that it should

never have happened. It was due to my own carelessness.'

He drained his glass and refilled it. 'But at least it brought me to my senses. I've been so bloody sorry for myself . . .' He shook his shoulders, as if he were shaking a burden from them. 'But let's leave all that for now and enjoy this moment and the splendid sunset the island's putting on for us.'

Anthea looked away from him through the window. The tall palm trees, silhouetted against the gaudy sunset, the lazy splash of waves and the thin song of a thousand insects. 'I'll remember all this when I get back to London,' she said. 'I'll be able to close my eyes and imagine myself back here.'

'You have to go back soon?'

'Oh, yes, very soon; there's my job waiting for me.'

He didn't know that there was no job waiting for her—he didn't know about the fire and the loss of all her stock and equipment. But now wasn't the time to talk about that. Perhaps later on she might. How wonderful it would be if they could really talk to each other, exchange confidences, break through the high wall he'd put up between them! She mustn't try to rush things; she had to wait. She said, 'It'll be lovely to have Pamela and Guy back in London again in a couple of months. I've missed them. Nancy and Bill will be the lucky ones—two years of this marvellous climate.'

Talk about their families took them through to the end of the meal. The sunset had given way quite suddenly to velvety darkness, but the stars hadn't yet appeared. Anthea closed the window against night insects and drew the curtains.

'That was a lovely meal—thank you,' Charles said as they settled down on the sofa with their coffee, having decided against brandy or liqueurs.

Anthea could find no reply. She seemed to hear the minutes ticking away in her head now. Had she been wrong in thinking that Charles intended to confide in her? He'd said, 'there are things I must tell you.' But perhaps he'd changed his mind.

The silence lengthened until she couldn't bear it any longer. 'You said——' she began.

'Anthea, I——' he said at the same moment, and they both laughed rather uneasily.

'Let me,' Charles said. 'I said earlier on that I owed you an explanation. At the beginning I laid down a lot of rules and you've been very sporting to accept them—I realise that it's not the usual thing to make rules about friendships.' His mouth tugged down at the corners.

'I was at the end of my tether when I arrived here. Just being with you has made life bearable. That sounds grudging, I know, but I'm trying to be honest.' He leaned forward, pressing his fingers against his forehead as if he was trying to push away a bad memory.

'You don't have to...' she began. She wanted to reach out to him, to tell him it didn't matter, whatever it was.

'Yes—listen,' he said jerkily. 'I must tell you about Mark. I want you to understand.'

'Mark?' Her eyes flew open wide.

'My cousin Mark,' he went on as if she hadn't spoken. 'When my parents were drowned we were staying with Mark's family in Australia. Afterwards, Nancy and I stayed on. Mark is an only child and his parents gave us a home. We were at school and university together. Mark and I were almost the same age—he was just a couple of years older. It was like having a twin brother—we shared everything. And when we grew up it was just the same—there was this strong bond. I'd have trusted him with my life—it was that kind of friendship.

'When the family moved back to England we had to decide what to do. It was taken for granted that whatever we did we'd do it together. I don't think either of us was wildly keen on any particular career, although we were both pretty good at maths. So when Nancy married Bill it seemed natural that Mark and I should go into the financial world too. We started our own company—with Bill's help—and we did well right from the start. Mark found he'd got a flair for handling people and for handling money. He was brilliant, I was——' he grimaced '—adequate. Life was exciting then. Parties, concerts, theatres, holidays, girlfriends. We worked hard and we played hard. I don't think we ever discussed it but it was sort of taken for granted that marriage wasn't an option that either of us contemplated.

'Then the inevitable happened: I met a girl—*the* girl. Her name was Elsa and she was quite the most beautiful thing I'd ever seen. I was crazy to get married straight away but she hung back—said she couldn't make up her mind to be what she called "tied down". Mark was away. His mother had died and his father had gone back to Australia. I couldn't wait for him to come back and meet Elsa.'

He said heavily, 'He came home, they met—and he took her from me.'

'Oh!' Anthea's soft murmur of sympathy was drawn out of her. There was so much she was beginning to understand. But she didn't think he was conscious of her at all now. He was living in the past.

His mouth was drawn into a bitter line. 'It was the stuff of which dozens of ham novels and plays have been written down the ages. That didn't make it any easier. I didn't . . .'

Suddenly he broke off. 'I think I'll have that brandy now, if Guy wouldn't mind.'

'Of course.' She leapt to her feet. 'I'll get it for you.' She went into the kitchen and brought glasses for them both. She was needing a drink too.

Charles was slumped back in the corner of the sofa. He looked desperately weary. She put the two glasses on the low table and went to the drinks cupboard. 'Water with your brandy?' she asked over her shoulder.

That was when the knock came on the front door— quick and urgent. Her first thought was Pam—something was wrong . . . the police . . . She ran to open it.

It was Nancy standing there. In the light that poured out from the hallway her face looked drawn, almost old. 'Anthea—is Charles . . . ?'

He came out of the living-room. 'Hello, Nan— what's up?'

Nancy stared at him, not moving. 'Charles—Elsa is here. She's just come and she's asking to see you.'

Then, out of the shadows, another figure moved forward. A girl in a black suit with huge frightened grey eyes. The girl Anthea had shared a taxi with from the airport.

'Charles—I've been trying to pluck up courage to come. Oh, Charles!' Her voice quavered, broke, and tears blurred her eyes and poured down her cheeks. As he moved towards her she threw herself into his arms, sobbing.

'All right, it's all right,' he said, stroking her shining black hair. 'Come along; you can tell me what it's all about.'

Without a backward glance towards Nancy and Anthea standing together on the step, he led the girl away.

'I knew it,' Nancy spat out viciously. 'I knew that girl would come back and spoil everything. I'm going to get rid of her. I won't have her...' She stumped after the other two, antagonism in every line of her solid figure in its brightly patterned cocktail dress.

Anthea went slowly back inside the apartment and closed the door. In the living-room she poured out, very carefully, a small brandy and sat down, sipping it slowly. But the blood had turned to ice in her veins and it would take more than brandy to warm it.

Moving like a zombie, she went into the kitchen, washed up the supper dishes and left everything spotless. In the living-room she put the furniture straight and plumped up the cushions on the sofa. One of them was still warm, where Charles's head had rested.

She laid her cheek against it, burrowing down into the sofa like a hurt animal. A long time later, when the cold started to eat into her bones, she crawled upstairs to bed.

CHAPTER TEN

AT TEN o'clock next morning there was a loud knock at the door. Anthea, who had just got up after an almost sleepless night, was in the kitchen, wrapped in one of Pamela's silk shifts, making tea.

She pushed back her hair, her heart thumping. Charles? Had he come to apologise for walking out on her last night—or to say goodbye?

But it was Nancy who stood at the door. She wore a creased red skirt and top and she looked as tired as Anthea felt.

Anthea summoned up a smile. 'Come along in, Nancy. I'm afraid I overslept—I'm just making tea; will you join me or is it too soon after breakfast?' Her voice was wooden with the effort to pretend that nothing particular had happened last night.

It was a relief to find that Nancy wasn't even making the effort. 'I haven't had breakfast,' she said wearily. 'I haven't been to sleep at all.' She followed Anthea into the kitchen and sat on one of the high stools, watching her make tea. When they were both seated, with the pot between them on the counter, she said, 'Charles has gone.' She looked ready to weep but instead took a swig of the hot tea Anthea had pushed across to her.

'It was awful. We had the most frightful row. I've never...' her lip quivered '...never quarrelled with Charles before. Not seriously.'

Anthea had always thought of Nancy as a reserved woman, certainly not given to emotional outbursts, but now she had started the words poured out. 'When he said he was going off with that girl, I told him...' she took another gulp of tea '...I told him what a fool he was making of himself. I begged him not to go—to stay and think things over—b-but he told me to mind my own business and said I'd fouled things up for him too often with my—my interference, and...oh, all sorts of beastly things. I've never seen him look so—so distraught. I was on my own—Bill was out with one of the bank officials.' She shivered, remembering. 'I was scared out of my wits. I've never seen Charles like that.'

Anthea listened in silence. Her world had begun to tumble down round her last night. This was the final collapse, and it was worse even than she'd expected in her darkest sleepless moments.

'That girl just hung on to Charles, weeping crocodile tears, putting on a great dramatic act. She never left him for a moment while he threw his things into a bag and went off with her in the car.' Nancy's indignation flagged and she seemed to droop. 'He must be out of his mind after what happened before—the way she let him down,' she said miserably.

Anthea swallowed hard to make sure her voice would work. Then she said, 'Has he—have they left the island?'

Nancy nodded. 'He flung it at me as they were leaving—said they were going on the first flight out this morning. I don't know where they stayed last night,' she added flatly.

She jumped up. 'There's someone at our door,' she cried and ran out to the front.

Anthea followed slowly. A coloured boy was riding away on his bike and Nancy was unfolding a letter.

She stood like a statue in the sunshine, staring at the writing inside. Then, without a word, she handed the note to Anthea.

'Nancy, dear,' it read in what must be Charles's strong handwriting, but scribbled hurriedly in a page torn from a notebook, 'I had to go. Please forgive. I'll be in touch. Charles.'

Anthea handed the note back to Nancy, who was looking weak with relief. Whatever foolish things Charles might elect to do, Nancy would never lose him.

'I'm so glad for you,' Anthea said. 'Perhaps he'll be happy with her in the end.'

'Perhaps,' Nancy said doubtfully. She looked hard at Anthea, who was suddenly conscious that her eyes were puffy and her cheeks drawn. She said, 'I'm sorry, Anthea. Charles was right: I should never have interfered,' and the brown eyes were kind and perceptive.

Anthea smiled at her. 'I've had a lovely holiday,' she said firmly. 'Something to remember. And Pamela's coming back today.'

That was really all there was to say.

Pamela and Guy arrived by the afternoon flight and Anthea was at the airport to meet them.

As she waited at the barrier her thoughts went back to this very place, twenty-four hours earlier, when the girl in the black suit with the haunted grey eyes had walked alone through the crowd, looking lost and frightened. The girl whom Charles had loved and lost and found again. Perhaps it was better that it had ended as it had—so abruptly—between herself and Charles. The girl had the fragile beauty that drew men to her like bees to a dew-drenched flower. Even another girl had to accept that, if she was realistic. Sadly Anthea acknowledged that she could never have competed with a girl who looked like that.

'Anthea, sweetie—you're here, how lovely! I can't hug you, I'm too horribly fat!' Pamela's silvery voice broke through Anthea's unhappy thoughts. They kissed laughingly and with due care, and, as Anthea felt Pamela's petal-soft cheek against her own and was engulfed in a cloud of Pamela's special scent, a little of her misery lifted.

Guy followed with the luggage and kissed Anthea too. Guy always seemed delighted to see her—he was the nicest brother-in-law—but she got the impression that his greeting was specially enthusiastic today.

Later, back at the condo, when they had exchanged news and eaten the dainty tea prepared by Juliana before she had left that morning, Pamela went reluctantly upstairs to rest.

'Only for an hour,' she declared. 'I want to hear about all the fun and games you've been getting up to while we've been away.' She cast a knowing glance towards Anthea.

'*Two* hours, my love,' Guy told her firmly as he led her upstairs. 'Remember...'

'What the doctors said,' finished Pamela, pulling a face at him. 'OK, but Thea must come up and talk to me while I'm resting.'

When Guy came downstairs again his face was serious. He poured himself another cup of tea and came to the point immediately.

'Have you made any plans about going back to London, Anthea?'

'I thought—early next week,' she said. 'It's been a shame to miss so much time with you and Pamela,' she added, and wished she didn't have to feel a hypocrite, 'but I've got a lot waiting for me when I get back.'

He nodded. 'Yes, I appreciate that, but the fact is, Anthea——' he smoothed back his already smooth fair hair '—well, the fact is I'm going to take advantage of your kind heart and ask you to stay on until the baby arrives.'

Oh, no, was Anthea's first thought. To stay on here where everything reminded her of Charles—it would be agony. But something in Guy's words made her go suddenly cold. 'Pamela...' she said urgently. 'She's all right, isn't she?'

Guy's keen eyes were fixed steadily on her face. 'Don't be alarmed, Anthea,' he said, and she had a crazy idea that this was how he'd look across his vast desk at the bank and tell a customer that he might be going to lose millions of pounds. 'But, you see, Pamela's condition is not quite...' he searched for a word. 'The doctors aren't a hundred per cent satisfied. They think that probably all will go well and that the baby will put in an appearance at the proper time. On the other hand, there's a certain risk that he or she may be in too much of a hurry to enter this wicked world.' His smile didn't reach his eyes. 'And if that happens there may be—complications.'

Anthea bit her lip hard. 'She's not—not likely to be in danger?'

He looked away from her, fixing his eyes on the distant lagoon, just visible through the window. 'I won't let myself believe that,' he said bleakly.

'Does she know?'

He shook his head and she could see a muscle in his cheek working.

Anthea had always liked Guy but at that moment she felt closer to him than she had ever done before. She said, 'Of course I'll stay, and do anything I can to help.'

He turned to her. 'Thank you, Anthea. Just be your own cheerful, sensible self. That'll do more good than anything. And if there's any way I can help you when you get back to London, you must call on me.'

Cheerful. Sensible. It wasn't going to be easy.

'Thea!' Pamela's voice called from upstairs. 'Come and talk to me.'

Anthea's eyes met Guy's and they exchanged a small smile. 'Coming!' she called back.

Pamela was lying against lace-trimmed pillows, looking gorgeous in a filmy blue chiffon wrap. She patted the side of the bed. 'Now I want to hear all about everything. And by everything I mean Charles, of course.' She smiled teasingly.

'Charles?' Anthea sat down, opening her eyes wide. 'What about Charles? He's gone back to London.'

'Oh!' Pamela looked put out and puzzled.

They had to get this thing settled straight away. 'Look, Pam,' Anthea said firmly. 'Charles and I went around together while you were away. He taught me to scuba dive and it was fabulous. He's an interesting man—when you get to know him—but there isn't anything serious between us. As I said, he's gone back to London and I don't suppose we'll meet again,

unless we bump into each other by accident. So don't
go getting ideas, Pam.'

Pamela's huge blue eyes looked hurt. 'I thought—
the way you spoke about him on the phone . . . I took
it for granted that you . . . I'm sorry, Thea, darling, I
didn't want to pry——' she bit her lip, pulled a lacy
handkerchief from under the pillow and mopped her
eyes '—being pregnant makes one very emotional.'

It was no good, Anthea thought. She couldn't be
any help to Pamela if she started off by putting a
whopping big lie between them. She sighed. 'OK,
Pam, I'll come clean. I fell in love with the man, but
it wasn't any good—he made that clear from the start.
He was in love with someone else—and she turned up
here yesterday. He went off with her last night. End
of story.'

'Oh, Thea . . .' Pamela looked stricken. 'I'm so sorry.
And here am I, selfish beast, weeping all over you.'
She blew her nose hard. 'Do you want to talk about
it?' she ventured.

Anthea shook her head. She was having a terrible
battle with herself to hold back the tears. 'Let's leave
it,' she whispered, and Pamela nodded
understandingly.

In the days that followed Anthea sometimes thought
that it would have been easier in London. London in
February, cold and cheerless, would have matched her
mood better than this glorious blue and gold paradise
island.

At first the pain was like a hidden enemy: she never
knew when it would strike, flooding her eyes with
tears, so that she had to turn her head away, biting
her lip savagely. But after a week it changed, eating

deeper into her, until it was always there, a heavy lump of misery, somewhere between her throat and her stomach.

The very worst times were at night in bed. She had said to Charles, 'I should have a memory,' and it was only too true, but she hadn't reckoned on the anguish of remembering the feel of his mouth, the heavy weight of his limbs on her, the clean masculine smell of him.

She tried to be rational about it, reminded herself that she'd known all along that it would be futile to hope—but when you were in love you couldn't stop yourself hoping. Lying awake in the small hours of the morning, she imagined Charles's coming to find her, telling her that it was all a mistake, that he wasn't in love with Elsa any longer, that it was Anthea he really loved.

But in the brilliant light of day she had to accept the truth. He had gone out of her life and he wouldn't come back. She told herself that one morning she would wake up and find that she'd fallen out of love. She'd heard that it always happened. But as the days passed she was still waiting for it to happen.

Most of the time she spent with Pamela, sharing old memories, discussing Anthea's plans for starting up her business again, talking about the coming baby, carefully avoiding any mention of Charles.

They sat out on the veranda when the sun wasn't too hot. Sometimes Anthea swam in the pool while Pamela lay in one of the green loungers and chatted to bank acquaintances. Once or twice, when Pamela was resting in the afternoon, Anthea agreed to play tennis with Peter and found that his game was every bit as bad as he had promised her. But he was a nice boy, and he even made her laugh now and again.

Nancy was a frequent visitor. She seemed to have lost some of her sturdy energy these days; her voice was subdued and if she still held firm opinions about everything she kept them to herself. Anthea guessed that she, too, was fretting about Charles, although she never mentioned him.

Pamela noticed it. 'It's funny that Nancy never talks about Charles,' she said one day, as she and Anthea were having their morning walk round the condo grounds.

Anthea stooped to pick up a pebble from the grass. 'Oh, I don't think she approves of his girlfriend,' she said. She took Pamela's arm. 'Do you think Guy would run me into George Town tomorrow, while Juliana is here? I could buy a sketch-pad and some pencils and start jotting down a few new designs...'

'Of course; why didn't we think of it before?' Anthea heard the pleased relief in Pamela's voice and knew she was telling herself that Anthea was 'getting over it'.

But Anthea wasn't getting over it. Sometimes she felt she was two people—the cheerful lively girl who laughed and joked to keep Pamela's spirits up, and the other Anthea who was conscious always of the hard lump of misery gnawing away at her insides.

Two weeks dragged by. Three. Three and a half. Guy was looking more confident. 'I think we may have passed the danger point,' he told Anthea. 'Pamela has to go in for her check-up today; I'm keeping my fingers crossed.'

The appointment was for eleven o'clock and Guy was coming home to drive Pamela to the hospital.

After breakfast she said, 'I feel full of energy today—I'm going to make some ginger cookies, my speciality. We can have them for tea when I get back from the hospital.'

It was Juliana's day off and the two girls had the kitchen to themselves. 'They're so easy; you just stick everything in the pan together—butter, sugar, syrup—and when it's all melted you stir in the flour and ginger.' Standing at the electric cooker, Pamela gave a running commentary. 'Pass me down the flour from that cupboard, there's a dear.'

It was as Anthea was reaching up to the shelf that she heard Pamela give a little gasp. She turned to see her bending over, a hand pressed against her stomach.

After a minute or so she straightened up. 'I thought . . . I don't suppose it's anything.' She went on stirring.

But before the cookies were made she said quietly, 'I think you'd better ring Guy and ask him to come home. I'll just sit down for a while. And if you'd throw a few things in a bag for me, just in case . . .'

Anthea heard the car as she finished packing a bag for Pamela to take with her. She ran downstairs with it as Guy was helping Pamela into the car. Anthea got in beside her and held her hand on the drive to the hospital, marvelling at Pamela's pluck. The twinges were coming more frequently now, but in between she managed to joke.

'Six weeks early—the stupid little darling! Or perhaps it's me who can't count. Oh!' She drew in an urgent breath and clutched Anthea's hand tightly.

At the hospital Anthea kissed her before she was wheeled away, with Guy, looking very pale, walking beside the trolley. Then there was nothing to do but

wait, and drink endless cups of tea, and try to keep
her spirits up. When, hours later, she saw Guy coming
towards her she jumped to her feet.

He was looking dazed. 'It's over,' he said. 'A little
girl—they say a perfectly normal delivery and
Pamela's OK, thank God. The baby's very, very tiny.'
Suddenly his voice broke. 'Anthea, my dear, you can't
imagine . . .' He put his arms round her and she felt
the wetness on his cheek. How wonderful, she
thought, to have a husband who loves you as much
as that.

Anthea slept well that night for the first time for
weeks, and next morning got up with a feeling that
the heaviness inside her was lifting at last. Juliana was
delighted about the baby and chattered away while
she shared a coffee with Anthea in the kitchen. Later
Anthea visited the hospital and saw Pamela, looking
radiant, and later Guy took her to peep at little
Elizabeth—named after Guy's mother—in her plastic
tent, looking very tiny and helpless.

'They have to use all these tubes and things for a
premature baby,' Guy assured her, very much the
knowledgeable father, 'but they're pleased with her
progress.' He sighed, gazing at his daughter. 'She's
beautiful, isn't she?'

Anthea looked down at the tiny, helpless little
human being with her wizened face, her minute hands
and feet that looked as if they'd been put into a skin
that was much too large for them, her scanty fuzz of
nondescript hair, and squinting blue eyes, and she
smiled with pure joy. 'Beautiful!' she breathed.

Pamela was to stay in hospital for a week and Guy
spent most of his free time with her. The baby would
be allowed home later, when she had put on the

necessary weight. Anthea visited each day, and Nancy accompanied her on the third afternoon.

As they drove back to the condo in Nancy's little red Toyota Anthea remembered what Charles had told her about his sister's having lost her own baby, and was moved to admiration by the way she had responded so generously to Pamela's triumphant motherhood. She had been full of obviously sincere pleasure that Pamela had come through so well, and that the tiny Elizabeth was holding her own.

'It will be so lovely to have a new baby living next door until Pamela and Guy leave for the UK,' she said. She paused and flicked a glance at Anthea. 'Have you decided when you're leaving us?'

'Very soon,' Anthea said. 'Guy's arranging for a resident nurse for the first few weeks after the baby comes home, so there won't really be enough room for us all.'

There was a silence. Then Nancy said, keeping her eyes carefully on the road, 'I had a long letter from Charles today.'

'Oh, yes?' Anthea said brightly. 'How is he?'

'He seems much better. He talks about coming back to see us quite soon, possibly next week.'

Pain shot through Anthea like a sharp arrow. 'Oh, yes?' she murmured.

And bringing Elsa with him of course. She felt panic rise inside her, churning round sickeningly. She *must* leave before Charles came back. She started to plan feverishly. Tomorrow morning she'd go to the hospital and explain—Pamela would understand, bless her...she would ask Guy to book flights for her...perhaps she could leave tomorrow...she could at least get to Miami, even if she had to wait there for a flight to London. She was hardly conscious of arriving back at the condo and saying goodbye to Nancy with thanks for the lift.

'You're sure you won't come in and have dinner with us later on?' Nancy was saying, and somehow Anthea was managing to refuse regretfully, with the excuse that she had started work on some new designs and wanted to get on with them.

She went straight up to her own room, and sat down on the bed, shivering a little. It was ridiculous to feel like a trapped animal; she really must pull herself together. Charles wouldn't be here until next week at the earliest—that gave her three days to make arrangements and leave in a civilised manner, not run away like a scared rabbit.

Slowly, to calm herself down, she took out her travel-case and began to pack in some of the things she wouldn't be needing again. The sun-dresses, the bikinis, the swim-suits—everything reminded her of days with Charles, of things they had done together. The white one-piece swim-suit she'd worn that on their last dive when he'd carried her up the stairs after the accident, and laid her on the bed—just here—and she had begged him—yes, *begged* him to make love to her. Hot tears of humiliation, and loss, and wretchedness, burned at the back of her eyes.

There was a tap at the door and she sprang to her feet. Nancy, of course. She mustn't see her weeping. She made a dive for the adjoining shower-room and swilled her face with cold water, calling out, 'Come in, Nancy, I won't be a minute.'

Picking up a fleecy small towel she went back into the bedroom, wiping her face. 'I was just——' she began and then her knees went weak and she clutched the doorpost.

Charles was standing at the bottom of the bed. His face was pale under what remained of the tan, and thinner, almost gaunt; there were dark smudges under his eyes, and she saw the desperate tiredness there. He said, 'Nancy told me you were here,' and then he didn't seem to have anything else to say.

Anthea's hands were shaking so violently that the towel dropped from her fingers on to the carpet. Charles stepped forward and picked it up, holding it out to her, and their hands touched.

'Oh, God,' he groaned, and somehow his arms were wrapped round her and he was kissing her with a terrible intensity, like a dying man in the desert who found water at last.

He said raggedly, 'I want to talk to you—can we go out somewhere? I don't find it easy to look at you standing in front of that bed, it——' there was a stark hunger in his face '—it puts ideas in my mind.'

Anthea was still reeling from that kiss. She allowed him to lead her down the stairs and across the condo grounds to the long stretch of white sand where the sea turned over in lazy ripples. The beach was almost empty in the early evening, only a few snorkellers swimming in the turquoise water. The sun was losing a little of its heat and a cool breeze touched Anthea's hot cheeks.

Charles took her hands in his and his eyes were like a dark flame. 'First of all, sweetheart, I can say now what I couldn't tell you before. You told me you loved me and you'll never know how much I longed to tell you the truth then. But now I can. I love you with all my heart, my darling girl, and if you can accept me with all the—er——' he smiled a little grimly '—the drawbacks I'll go into in due course, will you marry me very soon?'

Anthea found her voice at last. When a miracle happened you grabbed and hung on to it. She said faintly, 'Of course I will, tomorrow if you like. But—what about Elsa?'

'Elsa is past history,' he said.

'But——' Anthea began.

'No buts,' he said. 'What I thought was love bears no relation to what I feel for you. I longed for you every moment we were apart. I'm not even half alive when you're not with me. I don't know how I got through that dark time without you. I want us to be together for always.'

'I want it too,' she whispered. She put her arms round his neck and kissed him full on the mouth and felt the shiver that passed through him.

'I think we'd better walk,' he said. And, arms entwined, lovers now, they walked along the edge of the tide.

Charles said, 'I wrote to Nancy last week telling her everything, but the letter only reached her today. I was scared that you might have left and I was prepared to come after you to London at the crack of dawn tomorrow. I arrived here just before you and Nancy got back from the hospital. When Nancy told me about Pamela's baby and said that you were still here I think I rather overwhelmed the poor girl with my reaction. However, we won't go into that. What I want now is to finish the story I began that night when we were so rudely interrupted.'

Anthea nestled up to him, her head against his shoulder, glorying in the warmth of his body through his cotton shirt. 'You don't have to—not now,' she murmured dreamily.

'I think I do. I've put up so many barriers between us—I want to clear them away so that we can start our life together without any secrets from each other.'

Our life together. It sounded wonderful. Her eyes were misty with happiness.

'I told you about Mark and Elsa,' he began as they walked slowly along. 'For a time it was hell; I seemed to have lost them both. But after a while I managed to persuade myself that we could all still be friends.' He gave a bitter laugh. 'What a hope! They didn't want me—all that Elsa wanted was the high life, and Mark was besotted with her. So eventually I just bowed out. I know now what I didn't have any idea of at the time. Elsa demanded the lot and Mark tried to give it to her. He bought her clothes, diamonds, a villa in Majorca. God knows how much money he spent. He ran up debts that his income from our firm couldn't possibly have met. He gambled heavily and lost. Then he started to fiddle the accounts to cover his losses. We each of us had our own clients. The trouble was that he took the money out of the accounts of *my* clients, not his own.' He drew in a shaky breath. 'I still can't understand how he could do that to me. Not Mark.'

Anthea's heart twisted with pity for him. She reached up and touched his cheek. 'He was in love with her,' she said softly. 'They say that love is sometimes a kind of madness.'

He took her hand in a hard grip. 'Perhaps it is,' he said harshly. 'I loved Mark. Oh, not the sort of thing that still invites raised eyebrows these days. As a kid I loved him as a wonderful elder brother—hero-worshipped him, I suppose. He was dynamic, colourful, confident, popular—everything that I wanted to be myself. Even when Elsa left me for him I couldn't hate him.

'I kept myself busy and I had no idea what was going on . . . until Mark took Elsa on a luxury holiday to Acapulco—and they didn't come back. That was when it all started to come out. God! It was a ghastly time as the accountants and solicitors took over and unearthed the details one by one—all of them apparently pointing to my own guilt. Finally, when the situation became clear, a meeting of shareholders was called.

'I went out to Acapulco to see Mark, to plead with him to come back and help me to straighten things out.' He stopped for a moment and then went on, his face grim. 'I don't want to dwell on the next part. Mark had changed. He wasn't the Mark I knew. He looked me in the eye—and denied everything.'

He paused, and Anthea felt his body tense before he could bring himself to continue. 'I had a fortnight to put in before the shareholders' meeting. That was when I came here to the Caymans, to be with Nancy. I felt she was the one sane person in my world whom I could trust. But when I got here I couldn't bring myself to tell her about Mark. She thought that I was still depressed about losing Elsa. I let her think so. It wasn't true but it seemed the easiest way.' He laughed mirthlessly. 'Being Nancy, she tried to find a nice girl or two to take my mind off my troubles.'

Anthea said quietly, 'And that was when we met again.' So much was becoming clear. 'I think I can understand now how you must have been feeling.'

He bent his head and laid his mouth against her temple. 'There was something there between us right from the beginning, although I was so bloody awful to you.' He groaned. 'I had a terrible battle with my conscience. I knew I shouldn't involve you, but I couldn't help myself.' His arm tightened round her. 'You'll never know what you did for me, sweetheart. Just being with you in those two weeks restored me to a kind of sanity. Finally, I knew that what there was between us had to be put to the test. That last night I resolved to tell you everything and let you decide. Then—you know what happened.'

She nodded slowly. 'Your lost love came back to you.'

He gave a hollow laugh. 'It wasn't quite like that. She came to tell me that Mark was dead.'

'Oh, no!' Anthea pulled away from him, her eyes searching his face, wide with disbelief.

'Oh, yes,' he said heavily. 'I think he meant the Acapulco holiday to be a last glorious fling. When the money ran out he—took an overdose. Elsa couldn't cope and she turned to me for help. She found out from the London office where I was and got on a plane that same day. Eventually she arrived here with no money at all when she'd paid for her airline tickets. There was no time to make explanations—I had to go back with her straight away and take over. True to type, she didn't even wait for the funeral once the legal affairs were settled. She latched on to a Mexican millionaire staying at the hotel.' His voice was scathing.

'I thought...' whispered Anthea. 'I wish I'd known. Whatever happened, we'd have been together, to share it.'

'I was tempted,' he admitted. 'My God, I was tempted. I wanted to make sure of you. But I persuaded myself to do the decent thing. It wouldn't have been a very auspicious start to our married life if you'd had a husband in gaol.'

She felt the blood leave her cheeks. 'It wouldn't have come to that, surely?'

'It might well have done. It was a very nasty business—small investors defrauded. The courts don't look kindly on that kind of fiddle. Fortunately it didn't come to the fraud squad in the end. You see—it's difficult to talk about this, but you must know everything—Mark left a letter, admitting all he'd done, giving chapter and verse, absolving me. I threw in every last cent I had and the firm is being wound up. The shareholders came out of it reasonably well.

'There was a lot of clearing-up to do, but eventually my part was over and I could leave the rest in the hands of the accountant and the solicitors. My first thought was to get back to the Caymans and explain everything to Nancy and Bill and—most important—to find you again. It's been a hellish time since I left you, sweetheart. I can hardly believe that we're together and that I've found peace at last.' He drew her towards him and kissed her, a long, lingering kiss that made her whole body melt.

'You will marry me, my love?'

'Yes. Oh, yes, yes.' Stars shone in her eyes.

'Even though I'm practically skint and I've got to make a fresh start?'

'No problem. Fresh starts are exciting.'

'It shouldn't be too difficult,' he mused. 'I've got a lot of good friends. I think I may give the financial scene a miss this time.' He grinned. 'Do you need a manager for your thriving design business?'

She pulled a face. 'I'm afraid there isn't anything to manage.'

'No thriving design business?' he said in amazement. 'No sales to top stores? Paris? Rome?'

She shook her head. 'Not even a room to work in.' She told him about the fire and it didn't seem important any longer. 'All I've got is the insurance money on the equipment.'

'And you didn't tell me?'

She lifted her face to his. 'We've both been pretty cagey,' she smiled. 'But not any more.'

'No, by God,' he promised resolutely. 'From now on we work as a team—no secrets allowed.'

That was the cue to a long interval of bliss. When they finally managed to pull apart Anthea said, 'It'll be lovely to start afresh together.' Womanlike, she added, 'Where shall we live?'

He looked mysterious. 'We-ell, how do you fancy a cottage in Hampshire with a work-shop for you and an apple tree in the garden?'

'Mmm—lovely. What a wonderful dream,' she giggled.

'Dream nothing,' he said stoutly. 'It belongs to Nancy and Bill. They've offered it to me on a long lease while they're away from the UK.' He chuckled. 'This time I think I'll accept with thanks one of Nancy's little schemes on my behalf.'

Anthea shook her head incredulously. 'Heaven!' she breathed. She could see the apple tree quite clearly now. There was a pram beneath the branches. 'And Nancy *doesn't* scheme,' she added fiercely. 'She only wants to help. She's a dear and I'm very fond of her, and if it hadn't been for her we shouldn't have——'

He stopped the rest of her defence of his sister with a long, hard kiss. 'I'd have found you for myself; we were meant to be together. From the moment I walked out on to that balcony and saw a shy little girl in a pink dress my fate was sealed. But I'll allow Nancy a tiny bit of the credit. Come on, let's go back and tell her our news.'

The sun was setting and everything was bathed in a soft golden light. 'Just keep on saying you love me,' Charles demanded. 'Over and over again.'

She cuddled up against him as they sauntered back along the edge of the tide. 'I love you—love you— love you.' Her heart sang with happiness. 'From the moment you walked out on to that balcony...'

From the author of Mirrors comes an enchanting romance

PATRICIA MATTHEWS

Caught in the steamy heat of America's New South, Rebecca Trenton finds herself torn between two brothers – she yearns for one, but a dark secret binds her to the other.

Off the coast of South Carolina lay Pirate's Bank – a small island as intriguing as the legendary family that lived there. As the mystery surrounding the island deepened, so Rebecca was drawn further into the family's dark secret – and only one man's love could save her from the treachery which now threatened her life.

W●RLDWIDE

AVAILABLE IN JANUARY 1992 – PRICE: £3.99

The truth often hurts . . .

Sometimes it heals

Critically injured in a car accident, Liz Danvers insists her family read
the secret diaries she has kept for years – revealing a lifetime of courage,
sacrifice and a great love. Liz knew the truth would be painful for her
daughter Sage to face, as the diaries would finally explain the agonising
choices that have so embittered her most cherished child.

Available now priced £4.99

W♦RLDWIDE

TORN BETWEEN
TWO WORLDS . . .

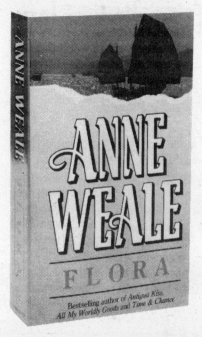

A delicate Eurasian beauty who moved between two worlds, but was shunned by both. An innocent whose unawakened fires could be ignited by only one man. This sensuous tale sweeps from remotest China to the decadence of old Shanghai, reaching its heart-stirring conclusion in the opulent Longwarden mansion and lush estates of Edwardian England.

Available now priced £3.99

W⬤RLDWIDE

From: Boots, Martins, John Menzies, W.H. Smith
and other paperback stockists.
Also available from Mills & Boon Reader Service, PO Box 236,
Thornton Road, Croydon Surrey, CR9 3RU

The burning secrets
of a girl's first love

Anne Mather

Hidden in the Flame

From the million-copy
bestselling romance author

She was young and re-
bellious, fighting the re-
strictions of her South
American convent. He
was a doctor, dedicated
to the people of his war-
torn country. Drawn to-
gether by a powerful at-
traction, nothing should
have stood in her way –
yet a tragic secret was to
keep them apart.

Available now priced
£3.99

W●RLDWIDE

4 FREE

Romances
and 2 FREE gifts
just for you!

*You can enjoy all the
heartwarming emotion of true love for FREE!
Discover the heartbreak and the happiness, the emotion
and the tenderness of the modern relationships in
Mills & Boon Romances.*

*We'll send you 4 captivating Romances as a special offer
from Mills & Boon Reader Service, along with the chance to
have 6 Romances delivered to your door each month.*

Claim your FREE books and gifts overleaf...

An irresistible offer from Mills & Boon

Here's a personal invitation from Mills & Boon Reader Service, to become a regular reader of Romances. To welcome you, we'd like you to have 4 books, a CUDDLY TEDDY and a special MYSTERY GIFT absolutely FREE.

Then you could look forward each month to receiving 6 brand new Romances, delivered to your door, postage and packing free! Plus our free newsletter featuring author news, competitions, special offers and much more.

This invitation comes with no strings attached. You may cancel or suspend your subscription at any time, and still keep your free books and gifts.

It's so easy. Send no money now. Simply fill in the coupon below and post it to -
Reader Service, FREEPOST, PO Box 236, Croydon, Surrey CR9 9EL.

NO STAMP REQUIRED

Free Books Coupon

Yes! Please rush me my 4 free Romances and 2 free gifts! Please also reserve me a Reader Service subscription. If I decide to subscribe I can look forward to receiving 6 brand new Romances each month for just £9.60, postage and packing free. If I choose not to subscribe I shall write to you within 10 days - I can keep the books and gifts whatever I decide. I may cancel or suspend my subscription at any time. I am over 18 years of age.

Name Mrs/Miss/Ms/Mr _____ EP18R

Address _____

_____

Postcode _____ Signature _____

Offer expires 31st May 1992. The right is reserved to refuse an application and change the terms of this offer. Readers overseas and in Eire please send for details. Southern Africa write to Book Services International Ltd, P.O. Box 41654, Craighall, Transvaal 2024.
You may be mailed with offers from other reputable companies as a result of this application.
If you would prefer not to share in this opportunity, please tick box. ☐

mps MAILING PREFERENCE SERVICE